CARNAL VENGEANCE

BOURBON DYNASTY

EVA CHARLES

QUARRY ROAD PUBLISHING

Letitia Hasser, RBA Designs, Cover Design

Dawn Alexander, Evident Ink, Content Editor

Nancy Smay, Evident Ink, Copy and Line Editor

Faith Williams, The Atwater Group, Proofreader

❧ Created with Vellum

Vengeance is a symphony of pain orchestrated by fate.

Vengeance in Death

— JD ROBB

ALSO BY EVA CHARLES

STEAMY ROMANTIC SUSPENSE

BOURBON DYNASTY
Carnal Vengeance
Tainted King
Scarlet Queen
Righteous Reign

A SINFUL EMPIRE SERIES
TRILOGY (COMPLETE)
Greed
Lust
Envy
DUET (COMPLETE)
Pride
Wrath

THE DEVIL'S DUE (COMPLETE)
Depraved
Delivered

A NOTE FROM EVA

WELCOME to the Bourbon Dynasty world!

Carnal Vengeance takes place during the Christmas season, but it's not your mother's Christmas novella. Trust me on this!

If you are new to my work, please know that I don't shy away from dark themes, ruthless characters, and language that will make your eyes bleed. Carnal Vengeance is no exception, and Bourbon Dynasty is **not** a safe series. But I do want you to feel safe. Please contact me with any questions or concerns before diving in.

Also, while Carnal Vengeance can be read as a standalone, it's a prequel novella, just the beginning of the new series. While it is a complete story—there is no HEA—yet.

Now that I've warned you away...

I am SO in love with all the characters in this new world (well, maybe not all), but I'm especially attached to Jake and all the layers and nuances that embody the man. He's mouth-watering in a suit and he made a killing on Wall Street, but make no mistake, Jake's a country boy through and through. He's also the most tortured hero I've written to date. His wounds are deep, and his sights are set on vengeance at any cost.

Is he redeemable? I'll leave that for you and Scarlet to decide.

For now, dangerous men, unfettered lust, secrets and lies await you...

I hope you love Carnal Vengeance!!

xoxo

Eva

1

JAKE

"I want you to set up surveillance in a speakeasy I'm opening next year."

Chase Wilder grabs a handful of spicy caramel corn that the waitress brought with the drinks. "Thought you were makin' bourbon on some estate outside of Lexington."

"I am." Although I'm not *just makin' bourbon*. I'm creating a brand that's going to destroy the competition. "The speakeasy is under the Wolf Trap distillery."

"Under the distillery. Really?" There's a gleam in his eye. Hard not to be excited about a secret club with the potential for all kinds of debauchery—and he doesn't even know the half of it.

"A previous owner went to great expense to build space underground where he could do business during Prohibition. It's an impressive setup. Just needed to be brought up to code, and now Jolie and Gil are working their magic."

If I didn't already have his attention, I have it now. Jolie and Gil are an architect and design dream team who did the over-the-top fantasy rooms at Wildflower, his brother Gray's club.

"This isn't actually a speakeasy we're talking about, is it?"

"It's more of a speakeasy than Wildflower is a dinner club." I pause. "We'll be offering cocktails with a variety of *entertainment* options. Something for every taste."

Ford, who appointed himself my personal bodyguard after he left the military, snickers from across the table.

Chase doesn't pay him any mind as he brings the drink to his mouth, wheels turning.

He's interested, but in the end, I'm not sure he'll be willing to take the risk.

I sit back with a tumbler of bourbon and stretch my legs while he mulls it over.

We're seated in the far corner of the bar, my back toward the wall, which I prefer in an unfamiliar setting. It minimizes safety concerns and normally allows for sweeping views of the room. But this place looks like Santa's elves vomited Christmas all over it, and the swanky clutter makes it impossible to see the entire room.

I despise Christmas. If I had my way, I'd be fallin' down drunk from the moment the first tree was lit until it became January kindling. But I don't have time to indulge my anger and resentment in that way. Besides, I have a better plan to soothe the regret that eats at my soul, especially at this time of year. With any luck, Chase is going to help me.

"You in?" I ask before he sets his glass down.

"Any fool can set up surveillance," he replies shrewdly. "Why me?"

"Your brothers claim you're the best in the business. Probably a bit of hyperbole sprinkled in their praise,"—his mouth twitches at the corners—"but they're not just proud papas. I've seen your work." I hold his gaze steady. "And I trust you."

"Santa Tell Me" plays softly in the background, while Chase cracks his knuckles. "Illegal surveillance?"

It's not exactly a question. He knows what I want, but I respond anyway, sidestepping the unsavory implications.

"Unlike Wildflower, the speakeasy isn't a front. It's a marketing tool—I'm selling exclusivity to build the bourbon brand. Everyone's fully vetted, members and guests. No one walks in off the street—ever—doesn't matter who they are."

Ford gestures toward the small silver bowl of caramel corn that's out of reach.

I nudge it closer to him and continue. "There's an annual membership with four levels of buy-in. The first three are what you'd expect, but the top tier gets you one of a dozen or so suites in a gated area."

Chase narrows his gaze. "What's the buy-in for the upper tier?"

"Seven figures. Although the first year we're comping a couple of those memberships."

"Let me guess, the freebies are going to powerful, well-connected men who might be a bit short on cash. Politicians, for example."

The sarcastic bastard is correct.

"Not all power is attached to a dick," Ford pipes up, knowing that I've already chosen the marks, and neither the governor nor the senior senator from Kentucky are women.

"You're planning to mine and record *behavior* that will allow you to, to..."

"Persuade individuals with real power to see things my way." I finish his sentence before he can come up with a more delicate phrase than *blackmail*. Folks from Charleston are far more genteel than those of us from Kentucky, at least the part of Kentucky I'm from.

"I'm not in the hunt to ruin anyone." *At least not anyone who'll have access to those rooms.* "But if it becomes necessary, I'll do *whatever* it takes to protect my interests. I'm not squeamish."

Chase is no Boy Scout, but his brow furls as he considers

toward the arched doorway that leads to the hotel lobby.
"Maybe you'll have a chance to get your dick wet tonight too."

Ford glances at the doorway and stiffens.

The man has an easygoing veneer, but he's a big, tough
dude who's faced his maker more than once. It takes a lot to
rattle him.

I turn my head, but a giant tinsel-clad tree obstructs my
view of the door. *Fucking Christmas.*

Discreetly, I inch the chair to the left, until I can see the
entrance.

2

JAKE

IT TAKES A MOMENT TO REGISTER—A long moment that plays out in slow motion accompanied by fuzzy vision and a head filled with nothing but white noise.

"What the fuck?" Ford mutters under his breath, as the hostess leads three young women to a table. A petite blonde and two brunettes, one of whom has my complete attention.

My gut churns like a son of a bitch while I watch her slide a shapely ass onto a velvet bench, then gather her long hair over one shoulder.

It's been nineteen years since I last laid eyes on her. She was reveling in life, and I was dead inside, on the threshold of hell.

I swallow the emotion before it sinks its claws into me.

This was not meant to happen—not like this. Nowhere in my meticulous plan is there a point where I encounter the enemy in a Charleston bar.

No. I'm the puppet master this time, and the mayhem is scheduled to unfold on my terms.

Yet here we are.

"Guess there's no law against vermin runnin' all over

Charleston." I throw back my drink and signal the waitress to bring another.

"You think she's here for the wedding?" Ford eyes me, cautiously. He's concerned, and if I had a lick of sense, I'd be concerned too.

"Gray wouldn't invite her," he adds, "but what about Delilah? Any chance they're friends?"

I shake my head. "No. It's a small wedding. I'd know if she was invited." *Gray would never let me be blindsided. Never.*

Ford pulls out his wallet. "Let's get out of here."

"Not yet. I ordered a drink and I'm not going anywhere until I've enjoyed it."

After the waitress takes their orders, the brunette who I've never seen before says something and they all laugh.

She shouldn't be laughing. She shouldn't be enjoying life. It's not right.

The anger rises inside, much the same way it did the night I saw her through the window, dancing near the Christmas tree like a sugar plum fairy. But this time, I'm not a helpless boy they can lock up to silence.

"Plenty of places in this town stock good bourbon." Ford's voice is tight. "We can get a drink somewhere else. It's a bad idea to stay here."

A very bad idea. "I'm full of bad ideas. You should know that by now."

"Jake," he pleads. But before he can continue, the waitress is back with my drink.

Ford can save his breath. I won't be driven away again. This time, I'll go when I'm ready. Until then, I'll observe, and squirrel away any useful tidbits I discover. Coming face-to-face with her in Charleston might not be part of the plan, but it could be an unexpected windfall.

"This isn't going to end well," he chides the minute the waitress is gone.

"Would you relax? There's no way she recognizes me."

I only recognized her because for the better part of two decades, I've been plotting to destroy her family—specifically, her father and grandmother. Otherwise, I wouldn't know her from a hole in the wall.

"I have no intention of derailing a plan that's been this long in the making."

"Bullshit. If that were the case, we wouldn't still be sitting here."

I glare at him. "Feel free to leave if it offends your sensibilities, sugar. But I'm staying."

Ford grunts his disapproval, but his ass doesn't leave the chair.

I sit back, bourbon in hand, and set my sights on the brunette who's much more attractive than she has a right to be.

"All the groundwork's been laid. Everything's ready to be set in motion. She had *nothing* to do with what happened." Ford's using reason with someone who's in no frame of mind to listen to reason.

Collateral damage. Maybe that should kick my conscience to life, but even on a good day, it barely has a pulse. "With those genes, I doubt she's an innocent."

"What could you possibly hope to gain from this?"

Don't know. Can't explain the pull. It's like my better angels took off and left me with a demon hell-bent on wreaking havoc.

I sip the bourbon, letting the rich notes dance on my tongue.

"Can I get you gentlemen anything?" the waitress asks, placing a fresh bowl of popcorn on the table.

"We're all set," Ford tells her. "Thanks."

Not so fast.

"Send those ladies, drinking champagne," I point to where the enemy lies, "a round of shots."

"What do you have in mind?"

There's a glimmer in her eye, like she's down for a little fun. But this has *nothing* to do with fun—not hers, not theirs, not even mine. It's strictly business.

"Got anything with the Langford label?"

She doesn't bat an eyelash. "We only carry Elk's Crossing. The fifteen-year reserve is all we have right now."

"It'll do."

Those fuckers have already taken plenty from me, and I'm loath to give them another cent, but this might just be worth it. "Put it on my tab."

"Of course."

"You're insane," Ford hisses. "What the hell are you doing?"

I gaze at the brunette who's posing for a selfie with her girlfriends. Something Willow never got a chance to do.

"I wanna play."

3

MADELINE

"Let's review the rules," Ariana announces, with feigned authority. The girl never met a rule she didn't want to break—or at least bend—and now she's making them.

"First," she ticks off her finger, "it's girls' weekend. Can't ditch your besties to get off with a hot dude." She snickers. "I meant *go* off."

Cassie rolls her eyes, and I bite the inside of my cheek to keep from laughing. Neither of us are going off with any guy, hot or not. For one thing, Cassie's happily married, and I'd never *go* off—or *get* off, for that matter—with someone I just met. Ariana, however, is a free spirit. It's terrifying at times, but it's also one of the things I love most about her.

"Don't worry about us," Cassie quips, spreading Camembert on a water cracker.

"I don't worry about you. But you," Ariana wags a perfectly manicured finger at me, "need to have some fun. Between work, taking care of your nana, and school," she adds in a whisper, because no one is supposed to know that I'm in business school. *No one.*

If it ever got back to my father—I'm not sure what he'd do.

Me with a business degree? He'd see it as a threat, and when his power's threatened, I wouldn't rule anything out. At the very least, he'll find some clever punishment to ensure I stay in my place.

A chill runs through me, and I rub both palms over my upper arms to get warm. *I need to relax.* We're far from home, and no one in this town knows me.

"You do need more fun in your life," Cassie adds softly. "Although with three girls under the age of five, I'm not one to talk."

They aren't entirely wrong. I have a number of commitments that eat up most of my waking hours. Yes, my life consists of a lot more work than play, but I'm not some poor girl to be pitied. I have resources and I own every decision I've made. *I wouldn't change a single one.*

"I'm here with my besties for the entire weekend." I lift my champagne flute to each of them, before taking a sip. "That's the best kind of fun."

"Your neglected vagina doesn't think so." Ariana dismisses me with a huff and goes back to the rules. "We can't go off with an imaginary hot guy, but shameless flirting is definitely on the table." She turns to Cassie. "Flirting's not off-limits if there's no touching involved, right?"

Cassie returns the cracker—inches from her mouth—to a small plate on the table and shoots Ariana a glare that would make a cactus wither. "If you caught Tyler flirting with some girl behind my back, what would you think?"

"I'd think the ice pick that I skewered his balls with was a good beginning."

Cassie snorts. "Flirting's out, but there's no harm in chatting with someone, while you two cocktease your way to giving some unsuspecting dudes blue balls. I'm down for that show."

Me too. Although I don't think there's going to be much of a show tonight. We chose this hotel because it's in a good spot for shopping and sightseeing, and it has a fabulous spa. We didn't choose it for the bar. It's lovely and safe, but a bit buttoned-up. We're only here because we were too lazy to go out after we checked in.

"I'm excited about the ghost tour tomorrow," Cassie says, taking a sip of champagne. "Do you think we'll see something?"

"No." I shake my head. "I read a bunch of reviews—"

"Of course you did," Ariana mutters.

"I think the best we can hope for," I continue, ignoring the good-natured jab, "is an eerie vibe or some weird sensation. But it'll be fun."

"You can't tell anyone that—" Before Ariana finishes, the waitress appears with three shot glasses filled with an amber liquid.

"We didn't order those," I tell her quietly.

"No," she replies, eyes twinkling. "But you definitely want them. They're Elk's Crossing Reserve. Fifteen-year."

The skin at the back of my neck prickles the moment she says *Elk's Crossing*.

My family's been making the storied bourbon for more than a hundred years. The reserve is one of the best—and costliest—bourbons on the market.

Someone must have recognized us—recognized *me*. Maybe the bartender.

No. The bartender didn't send them. No one who knows anything about bourbon does shots of fifteen-year-old E.C. Reserve. It's meant to be sipped and savored, not thrown back like white lightning.

"Who should we thank?" Ariana asks, casually scanning the room.

"The guys sitting at the table in the far back corner."

Cassie and I start to turn our heads.

"Don't be so obvious!" Ariana chides through clenched teeth.

When she's sure we're not going to do anything to embarrass ourselves or her, she turns to the waitress, who's more than a little amused. "Do you know who they are?"

She shakes her head. "They were here with Chase Wilder, the former president's son. He's gorgeous, and I hear he's a beast, if you know what I mean." She sighs. "But he left a little while ago, so we're all out of luck. Never seen the other two."

The mention of beasts has Ari sitting up straight, beaming, with an excitement swirling around her that's palpable. You can't predict what's going to happen next when she's like this. "What do they look like?"

"They're both good-lookin'. Real good-lookin'. One's kind of intense, broody, maybe preoccupied. The other seems more easygoing. I need to take an order," the waitress says, refilling my water glass. "Be right back."

"Elk's Crossing Reserve." Cassie whistles. "That's quite a coincidence. Think it's someone you know?"

Coincidence? *I doubt it.* Although I suppose it's possible they have money to burn and just wanted to show off by sending over the most expensive bourbon in the bar. Guys are like that—especially if they've been drinking.

With all the Christmas decorations, not one of us is in a position to get a good look at them without being caught. "I hope it's no one from home."

We live in a fishbowl, and I was looking forward to letting loose, a bit, without it becoming fodder for the town gossips and my father catching wind of it. Nothing wild. Just a weekend of not having to look over my shoulder before I open my mouth, and wearing whatever I want—like this showing-too-much-cleavage-for-a bar-in-December sparkly halter top.

I finger-comb my hair, letting it fall over my chest like a veil, to conceal some boob.

Ariana pulls out a jeweled compact and pretends to reapply

lip gloss while she checks out the guys. "This is how it's done, ladies," she purrs.

In another era, she would have been a femme fatale. "Can you see anything?"

"A little. I think she's right about them being good-looking, but they're too far away to know for sure."

"Do they look familiar?"

"Not to me," she murmurs.

"Are they young? Old?" I'm seconds from snatching the damn compact to see for myself.

"Not old. Definitely not old."

"Why doesn't one of you go over and thank them?" Cassie suggests, checking her phone.

There's no way I'm going over there.

"Let them come to us," Ari replies coolly.

That's a better plan, but I'm too impatient to wait, and too curious.

"I have an idea," I whisper as the waitress returns.

"Do you want me to thank them for you, or you want to do it yourselves?" She grins.

I nod at the shots. "Bring us two more, please. Then tell Mr. Broody and Mr. Easygoing that we can only accept their generosity if they join us."

The moment the words are out of my mouth, the butterflies begin to swirl. "Does that sound too much like a pickup line?"

"Not when you put it the way you just did. I'll go get the shots."

"You're a goddamn genius!" Ariana squees.

I feel more reckless than smart. "What if it's someone from home and they think we're hitting on them?"

"I really don't think it's anyone from St. Germaine, but if I'm wrong, it's our word against theirs." Ariana pops a cube of cheddar into her mouth.

With a stealth wink, the waitress drops two shot glasses at our table and saunters toward the back of the room.

"She might be more invested in this than we are," Cassie murmurs.

My heart's thumping so hard I hear it in my ears. *I don't know what's gotten into me, but I need to relax.*

Ariana would have recognized them if they were from St. Germaine. We'll have a little fun and never see them again. *That's all there is to it.*

Ari holds up the compact and steals a peek. "They're coming!" she chirps.

4

MADELINE

"LADIES," the tall, blue-eyed hottie drawls, flashing a dimple. "I understand we've been summoned."

His voice is a buttery timbre wrapped in a lazy twang, the kind rarely heard in St. Germaine. *My heart's still pounding, but I'm breathing again.*

He's a Southern boy, a local maybe, or from somewhere in the Carolinas. Perhaps even Virginia. Wherever he's from, they grow them big and charming.

I feel one of those stupid grins slide across my face, but it's not just me— Ari and Cassie are grinning too.

He must be the easygoing one. Although his friend, who's got lively eyes and muscle to spare, doesn't seem broody or preoccupied.

Nothing about them looks familiar. I've never seen either of them. *I'd remember.* The Elk's Crossing must be a coincidence.

The tension gathered in the pit of my stomach melts away as soon as the realization hits, and I flip my hair back, because there's no need for modesty. Fun is back on the agenda.

Not-Blue-Eyes slides into the banquette beside Cassie while the blue-eyed devil reaches for a chair from a nearby table. When he twists to grab it, it's impossible to miss how well his muscular ass fills out a pair of broken-in jeans—not the designer kind.

Maybe a few drinks with these two are just what I need.

He places the chair beside Ariana, directly across from me, and lowers himself to the seat.

The man is *all* male. The way he carries himself, the scruff on his jaw, and his hands—big and strong with nothing gentle about them.

"Now that we're here," Blue-Eyes smirks, "what are you going to do with us?"

I'm still thinking about his hands, and my mouth is too dry to form words. Although, as I contemplate relaxing my rule about leaving bars with strangers, my neglected vagina is feeling hopeful.

"Shots, of course." Ari rubs her palms together. "But if we're going to party, we should at least be on a first-name basis." She gifts Not-Blue-Eyes a flirty smile. "I'm Tate."

The lie glides so smoothly off her tongue it's jarring.

"Cassie," my sweet friend, who would never lie, says with a soft smile.

My turn. I feel like I'm playing truth or dare, with all eyes on me.

"I'm Madeline," I tell them, a current skittering through my veins.

"Madeline," Blue-Eyes murmurs, like he's about to do filthy things to me—filthy things I'll enjoy.

"Pretty name," he muses before turning to the table. "I'm Jake," he cocks his thumb toward his buddy, "and that's Ford."

"Are you guys from Charleston?" Cassie asks nonchalantly, like we're not dying to know.

"Nope." Jake's tone is dismissive. "Where you ladies from?"

He glances from Cassie to me, completely unfazed that he didn't say where he's from before asking about us. *Dog. I'll bet Jake is as fake a name as Tate.*

"Not from Charleston," Ari announces in an exaggerated way that pokes a little fun at Jake and makes us all laugh— including him.

"You're a troublemaker." His eyes twinkle as he peers down at her. "I like that in a woman. I suppose it was your idea to lure us here?"

"We wanted to say thank you." Ari's wily and doesn't miss a beat. "And we were too lazy to walk across the room. But I can't take credit. It was Madeline's idea."

Even though I'm not fair, like my mother, I blush deep and easily. Right now, I must be a ghastly shade of beet red. *I'm going to kill her.*

"Is that right?" Jake drawls. The playfulness he had with Ari is gone now, replaced with a heated gaze that settles on my skin like a warm blanket in July.

He's the intense one. I see it now.

"Invited, not lured." It comes out like a schoolmarm chastising the class roughneck on his imprecise use of language. "We wanted to thank you. It was the right thing to do." *Oh God.* I sound like an idiot.

When I get nervous, nonsense flows from my mouth at an alarming rate. I press my lips together to stop my gums from flapping.

Jake's gaze doesn't waver; if anything, it's more heated. When it becomes too much, I take a few raspberries off the cheese board and place them on a plate.

My hands tremble as I pick up the board to pass it. "Would anyone like some?"

No takers.

Cassie's making small talk about the weather, but I'm not really listening.

I'm no longer looking directly at Jake, but he's still studying me. There's an intensity, a fireball, at the center of all that beauty. I'm not sure what it's about, but I am sure that I wouldn't want to be standing too close when it explodes.

"Well, invited or lured, I'm happy to be here." Ford slaps the edge of the table with two hands. "But we should get to the shots. I think there might be an expiration date on them. Don't want good bourbon to go to waste. What do you say, Jake? We've got a long day tomorrow."

Ford's comment draws his friend's attention away from me. I feel it the moment it happens, and I'm of two minds about it. Part of me is relieved because he's the kind of man you'd warn your friends against, and another part is disappointed, because he's the kind of man you'd warn your friends against. *Yes, that's it in a nutshell.*

Something passes between the two men. I have no idea what they conveyed, but it seems significant. From the look she sends me, Ari noticed it too.

"I agree. It's a damn shame to let good bourbon go to waste." Jake raises his glass. "To all the people not from Charleston."

Everyone laughs but me, although I force a smile.

The package is charming, and alluring in *so* many ways, but there's something dark inside. It was right there earlier, in his eyes. So close, I could almost touch it.

5

JAKE

BY THE TIME I put down the shot glass, maybe before, even I know tonight's a mistake that's going to dog me.

She's not what I expected—not really. Sure, she's polished, but she's not arrogant like the rest of her family. There's even something kind about her, which pisses me off. I needed her to be a stuck-up bitch. Still do.

Although the biggest problem—my biggest problem—is the way she flushes when she's rattled, then averts her eyes like she can hide. *So innocent. So sweet.*

If she were anyone else, I'd enjoy teaching her to keep her eyes on me in those anxious moments. By the time I was done, her cheeks—all of them—would be a lovely shade of red. *Scarlet.* Same color as her skimpy top.

But she is who she is, nothing will ever change that, and I'd rather stick my dick into a barnyard animal than into a Langford.

"Not a fan of Elk's Crossing?" I taunt, glancing at her half-full shot glass.

"Some people—" the little troublemaker beside me starts,

but Scarlet gives her a look that shuts her up mid-sentence. I thought it'd take a gag to silence her.

"It's outstanding," Scarlet gushes, "but I'm more of a sipper than a shooter."

Of course you are.

There's a hint of something in her tone...not arrogance, but pride. Elk's Crossing, like the rest of the Langford label, is going to be a has-been soon enough, but it's garnered hundreds of awards and accolades over the years. Just another reason it's going to be so satisfying to bring it down.

She wets her plump bottom lip then runs her teeth over it.

Tate won't shut up about some insignificant matter that only concerns spoiled rich girls. She's tart around the edges, unlike her friend sitting across from me with that fuckable mouth—the enemy, I remind myself over and over, until there's not a single thought of a sweet, wet mouth milking my traitorous cock.

My chest rumbles, like something deep inside is working itself free. You'd think I drank enough tonight to keep the demons at bay, but no amount of booze placates them—especially at this time of year.

The best I can hope for is that the hooch knocks me out for a few hours, and I catch a short break. *Bullshit.* Nothing helps those demons.

I need air. Now. Before I say or do something that blows my plan to smithereens.

I stand, and Ford's on his feet in a heartbeat.

"We need to go," I tell no one in particular.

"Not before we take a selfie!" Tate holds up her phone while shaking her tits in Ford's direction. He catches her gaze and smirks.

We've been in this situation before, and if we refuse, aside from looking like assholes, which I could give a single fuck about, we risk that she snaps a picture without us knowing.

Sure, we can have it taken down from all platforms like it never existed, but it's a huge hassle and we can't always get it down before someone sees it. I've gone to great lengths to keep my face off the web, and I have no intention of allowing Tate, or whatever her real name is, to screw things up.

The best way to manage the situation is to control it from the start. In truth, it's the best way to manage any situation. No one knows this better than Ford.

"How about we use my phone?" Ford waggles his eyebrows.

"Why yours?"

Jesus, she's a pain in the ass.

"If we use mine, you'll have to give me your number so I can send you the photo. Then I'll have it. Forever," Ford adds, like a lying dog. She can get on her knees and suck his dick, and he's still not going to send her a damn picture.

Madeline's eyes glitter under the pendant light. She presses her lips together, trying to bite back a smile while her friend rattles off a series of digits for Ford. *So pretty. So sweet. So off-limits.*

My patience is paper thin, with gaping holes popping up faster than I can plug them.

"Okay," Tate squeals. "Let's do this."

We huddle together, me on my last nerve, but trying to remain civil.

When I end up behind the woman who coaxed my demons to the surface tonight, I don't move to another spot. I won't run from a Langford. But I don't touch her, either. Even I'm not that stupid.

Ford holds up his phone, and in a blink of an eye, we're done. Not a moment too soon.

"Good night, ladies." I notice my hands fisted at my side and shove them into my pockets. "Stay out of trouble."

"The photo?" Tate waves her phone in the air.

"I sent it. You don't have it?"

She shakes her head.

"The service in here has been spotty all night," Ford explains. "I'll resend it when I'm outside."

"It was nice to meet you," the enemy murmurs with a guarded smile.

Her eyes are the color of young bourbon, with a dark hue at the edges that matches her lashes. They were animated a moment ago, while she watched Tate and Ford flirt, but they're wary now, as if she picked up on my mood.

She's wise to be cautious.

I once intended on ruining her to get back at her family, but as my thinking evolved, so did the plan. In the end, I decided against dragging her into a mess that didn't belong to her. I'm rethinking that decision.

Seeing her here, with her friends, not a care in the world, is eating me up from the inside. I can't separate her from the rest of the family—or maybe I'm just pissed that she has a pretty face and nice tits, and that my cock went rock hard when she licked her lips and blushed. I want to punish her for it—for all of it.

6

JAKE

"THE FIRST TEN minutes or so, I was prepared to give you a goddamn Academy Award," Ford grouses after the bellman pulls the door shut behind us, "but then you started looking at that girl like you wanted to destroy her with your dick."

With the windchill, it's below freezing, but it doesn't do a damn thing to cool the rage simmering inside. "I don't want to fuck her, if that's what you're implying."

"I'm not implying shit. I'm telling you straight up what I saw with my own eyes."

His SEAL training taught him to be more observant than most, but he isn't a fucking mind reader.

We pause at the curb to let a car pass. "Maybe you're seeing things. You've been hittin' the bottle hard since we got to Charleston. Besides, even if I did want to fuck her, and I don't, it would never happen. My dick would wither before it got anywhere near Langford pussy."

Ford's jaw tightens. "Keep telling yourself that if it helps you sleep at night, but it's not how I saw it."

He's accused me of dishonoring my sister—staining her memory with a meaningless fuck. *Son of a bitch.*

The rage inside explodes, shrapnel slicing through my chest wall. Before I realize what's happening, I have one hand around his throat and the other fisted in the air, ready to strike. It's only the wail of a passing siren that pulls me back.

I freeze, fist cocked midair.

Ford hasn't ducked, or tried to shake me off, or even raised an arm to block the punch. His feet are planted and he's staring right at me like he can see into my soul.

"Go ahead. You want to relieve some of the pain, take the swing. But it won't make you feel any better."

We've been tight since we were sixteen, and he knows me better than most anyone. The asshole's right. Even if I landed the punch, I'd still be raw inside.

I drop my hand, and we cross the road like nothing happened.

"It's early," he mutters. "You want to grab something to eat before we go back?"

"You go ahead. I'm going to walk along the ocean for a bit. I need to clear my head."

"I'm always up for anything that involves saltwater."

With the edge of my boot, I kick a stone off the sidewalk, so no one trips on it in the dark. "Don't need company."

"You do. You just don't want it." He pauses. "But before you go off half-cocked, you're going to hear what I have to say."

I drag in a long breath to stop myself from flipping him off and walking away.

"She got under your skin tonight. It was a massive pothole that you managed to steer around without any damage. Leave it at that. Bad things are going to happen if you write her into the plan at this stage." His voice is low and thick with emotion. "The kind of bad things that will send you to prison."

I'd rather be dead than go back to prison. "Not this time."

"Maybe you're right. Maybe not. It's a crapshoot, J. Do you really want to take that risk?"

I could say, *of course not*, and even make it sound believable. But I don't lie to people I care about, so I say nothing.

"Everything's in place. I'm behind you a hundred percent. You're going to bring down the bastards, fair and square. No more detours."

Even on a good day, I don't have the patience for well-meaning lectures, and today is *not* a good day. *If I have to listen to his shit for one more minute, I'm going to raise my fists and this time I won't stop until we're both bloodied.*

"Good night." Without another word, I turn and stride toward the Battery, where the Atlantic skirts the city.

When this started, she was the pawn that would bring down the entire board and get justice for Willow. I planned to settle up with the judge separately, because that was a connected, but different matter. That was about justice for a boy who'd been sent to an adult prison just weeks after his fifteenth birthday.

But after the McCaffreys took me in, I softened toward her. Maybe it was because I felt safe—protected—that can make anyone soft. Or maybe it was the love and guidance the McCaffreys so freely gave me, and the need I had to make them proud in return.

When I saw her today—*Madeline*—it brought me straight back to the night of the fire. The night I stopped to pull a little girl from the embers. I saved her, when I should have been saving my sister.

That night was the beginning of the end, but not the last time I laid eyes on the girl. I saw her once more, like an omen, right before I plummeted to the bottom.

Ford's right. I need to put her out of my mind and stay the course. Otherwise, seeing her tonight will become nothing more than a harbinger—just like in the past. I feel it in my bones.

I approach the Battery from the residential side. It's quiet.

Just me and the shadows created by the bone-chilling wind and the harvest moon. I flip the coat collar to shield my neck and bury my hands in the satin-lined pockets.

Put her out of my mind? Don't see that happening. There's not a single fucking brain cell willing to cooperate.

I can't stop thinking about her—her beautiful face with those warm, gentle eyes. Fuck me.

I won't be impulsive, because that's how mistakes are made, but I won't be soft, either. I'll do what I have to do—like always.

If I decide not to ruin her to get revenge, something even an asshole like me knows is despicable, I can still exploit her to get answers that have been a long time in coming. With a little manipulation, she can help me access information that I might not be able to get in any other way. Not even with Chase's help.

I'm still undecided about how to best use her—because I *will* use her—when I slide the phone from my pocket and make the call.

7

JAKE

"You better be seconds from death with no one else to save your sorry ass," Chase grunts into the phone.

It took three tries, before he finally answered. His breathing is choppy and his voice hoarse. I don't need to ask what he's doing. "I'll only keep you a minute."

"Start talkin'."

"I want you to find out everything there is to know about a woman. I mean everything. What she eats for breakfast, her favorite color, the name of every guy she's let touch her tits. No detail is too mundane."

"This couldn't wait until morning?"

"No, it can't wait until your little dick is tired and happy."

"Fucker," he mutters.

"She's in Charleston for the weekend with some friends. I want to know their plans, when and how they're leaving, and if they have security with them. I need that info immediately. The rest can wait until you come up for air."

"I'll be right back," he murmurs to someone who is not me. His voice is muffled, but I get the gist. "Don't you dare move that gorgeous body. Not a muscle."

I snicker. "If you tie them to the bed, they can't go anywhere."

A door creaks right before he sneers. "Is this some random chick you saw on the street? Because I'm not a fucking miracle worker."

"Not a random chick. I'll send you what I have on her. At least enough to get you started."

"I want the top-tier membership in that speakeasy for a year."

"You haven't done shit yet. Talk to me when you've earned it."

"Oh, I will," he snarls. "Gotta go."

"Chase."

"What?"

"This stays between us. No one else needs to know about it."

"Not even Ford?"

He's probing, but I'm not inclined to provide details. "Not even Ford."

Eventually, I'll tell him, but not until I decide how to proceed. For now, I've had enough of his chiding and pleading. Begging is a bad look on a big dude.

I end the call and shove the phone back in my pocket.

Some men prefer to take—no holds barred, no apologies—a partner's wife, a competitor's business, a ripe peach out of a hungry child's hand. Doesn't matter what it is or the harm it will cause.

At times I operate that way too, but with my kind of power and means, taking is easy. *Too easy.* I'm a sportsman at heart, and I live for the adrenal rush that comes with stalking prey—the hunt, the chase, and the surrender. I love it all.

Any plan that involves getting close to *Madeline* will have to include coaxing and cajoling. *Seduction.* I'll have to play nice.

Normally, I'd be all in. Once I set my sights on something,

I'm a man who'll play almost any game to get what I want. But I'm not sure I want to *play nice* with her—taste her mouth, lick her cunt, bury my cock inside her 'til she screams—even if the prize is justice.

I'm not convinced I have the temperament or the stomach to do what it'll take to seduce the enemy—*that* enemy. The thought of cozying up to her makes the bile rise in my throat. But I can't pass up the opportunity for a windfall that will lead to justice for Willow. I *won't* pass it up.

We'll have to see just how strong my stomach is.

8

MADELINE

"I can't believe that asshole didn't send the photo," Ariana grumbles, reaching over me to drop her phone on the nightstand.

When we got back to the room, Ari and I collapsed on one bed, and Cassie curled up in the other and immediately passed out.

"Maybe he entered a wrong number or forgot to resend the photo when he got outside." I keep my voice low so as not to wake Cassie. "They didn't seem like the type who would go to all the trouble of taking your number and posing for the camera just to be nice."

I didn't pay close enough attention to Ford to say for sure, but Jake certainly didn't seem like the type who goes along to get along. If anything, he seemed like a man who set the rules and expected everyone else to get in line.

"Maybe they thought we'd put it on social media," Ari murmurs. "A lot of guys hate that. There could be a girlfriend or a wife somewhere and they didn't want to get busted."

"Still doesn't explain why they went to so much trouble.

They could have just said no or made up an excuse. They didn't owe us anything."

"They're players. That's what players do. What I don't get is why they sent us those expensive shots and came over to our table, but neither of them made a single move. When guys send drinks, they want something in return—married or not."

"Maybe when they came over, they decided we were weird or too young."

"When has that ever stopped a guy who's already made an investment?" Ari asks. "And weird or too young is a perfect hook-up with a woman you're never going to run into again."

"Shit," she hisses, throwing off the comforter. "I forgot to brush my teeth."

I nudge her with my foot. "Go. I don't want to sleep beside someone with dragon breath."

Ari gets out of bed and fumbles her way through the dark hall and into the bathroom. She bumps into something and curses, but Cassie doesn't stir.

I don't think I've ever forgotten to brush my teeth before bed. I've never hooked up with a guy I just met, either. Freshman year of college, before my father summoned me home, I had a couple of hot make-out sessions after the bars closed. But they weren't sizzling enough for me to go home with a stranger I was likely to bump into in class or the campus dining hall.

"Jake was into you," Ari says while settling back into bed. "Big time."

"Stop hogging the covers." I tug on the bed linen. "Don't be ridiculous. He wasn't into me."

"He was the Big Bad Wolf, and he wanted to eat you, Little Red Riding Hood," she growls, until we're both giggling. "It's a shame. He's just what you need on a long, chilly night."

"Thanks a lot. You said yourself they were players...now you're lamenting the fact that I didn't have sex with him."

"Nothing wrong with a player as long as you see his game coming. But I'm telling you, a night in that man's bed and you'd be a new woman."

Doubtful. Sex hasn't been bad—not awful, at least—but it's never been life-changing, either. Even if this was somehow different, *new* doesn't always mean better. *Although if anyone could rock my world, it would probably be someone like him.*

"If you thought he was so great, why didn't you make a move on him?"

"He wanted you, not me. Besides, Ford's more my style. Easy. Laid-back. The kind of guy who lets you climb him like a tree. I did everything but reach for his belt. I never beg."

"His loss."

"Damn straight." She chuckles, but it's hollow. Ariana's bravado often hides shaky self-confidence.

"I think Jake's a take-charge kind of guy," she continues. "I doubt vanilla is his favorite flavor."

My pussy tingles at the thought of doing *anything* not remotely vanilla with someone like him. I've never dipped my toes into that pond, although I've wondered what it would be like to be blindfolded or tied up during sex—nothing too crazy.

I pull the comforter around me and tuck it under my chin. "Something about him was—I don't know—scary."

Ari turns onto her side, facing me. "You see every man who shows any interest in you as a potential threat or too flawed."

It's a harsh assessment, and it stings.

"I'm not judgmental."

"Only about men who like you."

"That's not true," I reply, but I know she's right. I've analyzed it to death. I won't become my mother, who married a man who only cared about how she looked on his arm. My father hasn't spoken a kind word to her since the wedding—maybe before.

I don't have my mother's delicate features—the kind of

classic beauty that men fawn over. But when my father dies, I'll inherit a well-respected and highly lucrative bourbon company. Langford is the darling of the industry. Always has been.

For many in the bourbon business, and for others trying to break in, my Langford shares are worth more than a pert nose and high cheekbones. *Far more.*

Ari doesn't argue, but I hate being called a snob.

"It's not that I don't think they're good enough. I'm not built for a night in a stranger's bed."

Trust is *always* a factor for me. Meet a guy, spend some time getting to know him, then take my clothes off.

"You need to stop sizing up hot guys to determine if they're relationship-worthy. Size them up to see if they'll be a good time instead. That's what they do with us."

Is that what I do? Assess men as potential partners? *Probably.* I suppose it's better than being a snob.

"Think of a hot guy like a platter of barbeque." Ari's eyes are closed, but even in the dark, I see the outline of an impish grin.

"Barbeque?"

"Mmhm. As long as there are no bugs crawling on it, dive in headfirst, inhale the entire thing until every juicy morsel is gone—lick every delicious drop off the platter. Enjoy the hell out of it, until you're so stuffed you don't want to see it ever again. One and done."

"That's a terrible analogy."

"I know, but I'm starving, and I can't stop thinking about lunch tomorrow. I've been dreaming about Felix's Barbeque since the last time we were in Charleston. The brisket is perfection. And that corn pudding. Oh. My. God. It's orgasmic." Ari's stomach rumbles, and we pull the covers up over our heads, so Cassie doesn't hear us cackling like hyenas.

"I have some nuts in my purse, or we could call room service if you're really hungry."

"No. This bed's too comfortable and I'm too tired to get up

again. Plus, if I don't eat tonight, I'll feel so virtuous when I wake up."

I smile. "Wouldn't want to rob you of that virtuous feeling. Good night."

"Night."

Not more than a minute passes when Ari murmurs, "I bet his meat's mouth-watering."

"What are you talking about?"

"Jake."

I snicker. "You're slaphappy. Go to sleep."

"Have a taste and report back."

"We're only here for two more nights, and Jake's probably not even his name. We'll never know what he's packing." *Now we're both slaphappy.*

"A girl can dream," she mumbles, half asleep.

Yes, a girl can dream. No harm in dreaming about those startling blue eyes that see everything. They penetrate more deeply than any cock ever could.

I doubt vanilla is his favorite flavor. I agree.

He gave off all kinds of bad-boy vibes...and some bad-man vibes too.

The more I think about him, the more restless I become— and the more aroused. But there's something else too. An almost eerie sense of heightened awareness that I don't understand and can't explain.

I don't need to explain it. I'll never see him again.

Still, the feeling weighs on me, and even though I'm exhausted, sleep doesn't come easily.

9

JAKE

WHILE THE BRIDE and groom are taking pictures after the ceremony, I'm able to corner Chase while he's hitting on a cute little waitress in an alcove under the stairs.

"He's trouble." I wink at the young woman. "But I'm here to save you."

She giggles nervously.

"I'll find you later, Molly."

"Polly," she calls, over her shoulder as she hurries away.

"That was smooth. *Molly*." I shake my head. "You could use a master class in seduction."

"Fuck you," he mutters.

"Thanks for the information. I know you have a lot going on. I appreciate it."

"Was it useful?"

"Very. But I do need one more thing from you before the day's over."

His nostrils flare. "You do realize that there's a wedding reception I need to attend. I think they're expecting you there too."

"Wouldn't miss it for the world, and you're not going to miss a minute of it either." Marriage isn't for me. I have too much baggage—too many festering wounds. No woman deserves that shit. But Delilah makes Gray happy—happier and more relaxed than I've ever seen him, and that makes me happy.

Chase scratches his head and grunts. "What do you need?"

"I need you to cancel her flight to Philly."

His body is rigid. "You're kidding, right?"

"I am not."

"You want me to hack into the FAA server and ground a goddamn plane?" He asks like he hasn't hacked into government servers hundreds of times.

"Of course not. I want you to hack into her email and cancel her ticket, then intercept whatever notices the airline sends."

"Is that all?"

Chase used to be a quiet, deferential kid, but he's a sarcastic bastard now. For the most part, I like the change. It suits him.

"Since you asked, I need the name of someone who can set up cameras in a suite at the Blackberry Inn. Need it done by noon tomorrow."

"You're looking to set up cameras in her room?" His voice is tight with disapproval, as his eyes bore into mine.

"In my room."

"Most guys turn to the web when they wanna rub one out. You have heard about internet porn, right?"

I glower at the little prick.

"I have no fucking idea what you're planning for that woman," Chase continues, "but I don't like the sound of it."

Ordinarily, I wouldn't like the sound of it either, but there isn't a line I'm not willing to cross when it comes to the vengeance I'm seeking.

"How far were you willing to go to get justice for your brother Zack? For Sera? Your mother?"

Sera and his mother were murdered, and there's not much left of his twin, Zack. It's a low blow, but I want him to understand that this isn't some sex tape I'm making to get off on later. It's bigger than that—*much bigger*.

Chase sighs and it's heavy with the knowledge that the answer is *as far as it took*.

"Justice is a lot less satisfying than you think, Jake. It doesn't change shit." He pauses. "I'll set up the cameras first thing in the morning, before the brunch."

I shake my head. "I don't want to take you away from the celebration any more than I already have. The job doesn't require your level of skill. But I appreciate the offer."

It would take Chase ten minutes with one hand tied behind his back, but I still have no idea where this is headed, and I don't want him involved. Hacking into her email is one thing, but this is something else entirely.

My soul is already irreparably stained. This is just one more pit stop on the road to perdition.

I'm the devil. I'm not afraid of the fire.

10

MADELINE

"You room won't be ready for at least a couple of hours." The clerk at the reception desk is apologetic, almost sheepish. "Just one moment and I'll get a bellman to take your bag."

While I wait for someone to collect my bag, I step away from the desk so she can help an elderly gentleman.

This is like déjà vu, only without Ari and Cassie, who should be home by now. I still don't believe I canceled the ticket, but the airlines love to pass on responsibility whenever they can so that they don't have to compensate passengers. Fortunately, when I explained my predicament, the hotel was able to accommodate me for an additional night.

"Madeline." The sound is muted by the noisy lobby, and I don't pay much attention to someone calling Madeline. *Why would I?*

"Madeline?" *The voice is familiar.*

I turn my head and a tall man with broad shoulders and piercing blue eyes is standing close enough to touch.

Madeline. Oh God.

"Jake. We met in the bar Thursday night."

I must look as flustered as I feel, but I'd never forget that face. *Those eyes.* "Yes, of course I remember you."

"Where are your friends?"

"On their way to St—on their way home." That was close. Although I suppose it wouldn't be the end of the world if he knew where I lived.

"Without you?"

He asks a lot of questions, and listens carefully to the answers, like I'm the only person in the cavernous lobby and what I have to say is of the utmost importance. I need to be mindful, or I'll be caught in a lie. *Not that it matters, although I would hate it.*

"I'm going to Philadelphia for a conference."

I am going to Philly, but not for a conference. That's what I told my father, and everyone, really. The only people who know the truth are Ariana and Cassie. I have a meeting with my advisor from the MBA program. *Had* a meeting. Hopefully Professor Evans reads my email and can reschedule.

Jake glances at my suitcase. "Are you on your way to the airport?"

I'm about to say yes, but I've already told enough lies and it's exhausting trying to keep it all straight. Why do I care if he knows I'm staying at the hotel?

"No." I shake my head. "My flight was—canceled. Not my flight, my ticket. I don't know how it happened, but when I checked in yesterday, I must have inadvertently canceled my ticket." *I'm blabbering again. It's so embarrassing.*

He nods sympathetically. "That's too bad. Will you miss the conference?"

"I'm trying to reschedule."

"The conference?"

Oh my God.

I laugh nervously. "No one's rescheduling a conference for

me. But I was meeting a colleague, and I'm hoping to reschedule with him."

One side of his mouth curls. It's not exactly a smile, but it's enough to flash that sexy dimple. "Got it."

He's relaxed today, the way he was when he first came to the table the other night. There's none of the devilish charm, but there's none of the intensity, either.

Maybe I imagined the intensity. Or maybe Ari's right. Maybe I always look for threats and flaws in men.

"Are you meeting someone in the hotel?" I ask, mostly to make conversation so he doesn't leave just yet.

He's gorgeous—every inch of him uber masculine, with strong features and a defined jaw. He hasn't shaved recently, and the shadow on his face is somewhat darker than his golden-brown hair. *I'm not ready to say goodbye to him.*

"I'm staying here," he replies, running the back of his hand over that sexy scruff. "I was in town for a wedding, and I'll be here for a few more days on business."

I want to ask what kind of business, but I don't, because it'll open the door for more of his questions and I don't want to tell any more lies.

From the corner of my eye, I see the bellman approach.

"Just one bag, miss?"

"That's it."

"I can hold the luggage until you collect it, or I can take it to your room when it's ready. What do you prefer?" he asks, holding out the luggage tag.

Before I can answer, Jake takes the tag from the bellman's hand and slips him a few bills. "We'll be at the bar. Bring it to the room when it's ready, and make sure there's water and plenty of towels."

Jake turns to me. "Do you need anything else? Ice?" He takes over so casually that it takes a moment before I'm taken aback by how forward he is.

"No." I smile at the bellman. "A few extra towels and water would be nice."

Before he leaves, the bellman glances at the bills pressed in his hand and thanks Jake. The outer bill is a twenty. That alone is more than enough for taking one piece of luggage to my room and placing a call to housekeeping for supplies. Maybe he's in the holiday spirit.

"You really didn't need to tip the bellman. I would have done it." *I'm capable of getting myself water and towels too.* My tone isn't snippy, but it's not exactly gracious, either, and it wasn't meant to be.

"I was raised by a Southern woman who believed gentlemen should spare ladies all mundane matters. But I have no doubt you can take care of yourself."

It's an attempt to smooth ruffled feathers, and it succeeds, although *gentleman* seems much too refined a word to describe him.

"And you're a gentleman?" I tease.

"Not even on my best day. Don't you dare rat me out."

He gifts me a smirk that makes my heart beat faster, and eviscerates all thoughts of pushy behavior.

"Your secret's safe with me. Thank you for taking care of the essentials." He nods but doesn't say anything, and I don't have anything to add that might keep him here.

"I'm off to explore the hotel a bit," I continue, before it gets awkward, "until the weather clears and I can take a walk."

"It's going to sleet all day and there's a roaring fire in the bar. If you want to thank me, let me buy you a drink." He pauses. "I could use the company."

I could use the company. It feels sincere, more like an honest admission than a pickup line.

The truth is, I could use a little company too. *Especially his kind of company.* I would be a fool to turn down the invitation. *Ari and Cassie would throttle me, and I'd deserve it.*

It's just a drink.

I gaze at him and smile. "You had me at roaring fire."

11

MADELINE

"Where's Ford?" I ask while Jake holds open the door leading to the bar.

"You were hoping to see Ford?" His gaze narrows, but there's a playfulness about it. "I'm crushed."

"You were looking for company, and I wondered where your sidekick went. That's all."

"He left this morning."

"Guess I'll have to settle for you." My smile is broad, and the warmth in my cheeks feels like I drank too much, although I haven't had a drop of anything stronger than the dark roast latte at breakfast.

When we enter the bar, the hostess asks to take my coat.

I start to take it off, but Jake steps in immediately. His knuckles graze the skin at the nape of my neck when he slides the coat off my shoulders. I shiver at his touch, and silently curse myself for being so obvious.

I'm not sure Jake noticed my reaction, but when he gives the coat to the hostess, I rub my hands together, pretending to warm them. It's a weak cover, but I don't want him to think I'm affected by his touch. "I don't remember it ever being so cold in Charleston."

"My buddy who just got hitched said hell would freeze over before he took a wife. Maybe that explains the uncharacteristic cold."

I roll my eyes, and he places a strong, steady hand in the small of my back and leads me to the far corner of the bar that's decorated to the hilt. The entire hotel feels like a winter wonderland. It's gorgeous.

When we stop, there's already a crystal tumbler with a generous pour of amber spirits on the copper bar.

"I stepped out to take a call," he murmurs, pulling out a leather stool for me, "then you waylaid me."

"I waylaid you?"

"Something like that," he murmurs, smirking.

A bartender wearing a Santa hat puts a napkin in front of me. "What can I get you?"

I cock my chin toward Jake's drink. "That looks tempting. Bourbon?"

"Yes, ma'am."

I nod. "Sounds good."

"Not interested in the label before you order?" Jake asks, raising an eyebrow.

It's an interesting way to phrase the question. Most people would use the word *brand* or *kind* instead of *label*. He did neither, which tells me he knows a lot about bourbon and its culture. Which, in turn, makes me especially curious that he sent us shots of Elk's Crossing Reserve the other night. The fifteen-year, no less. But there are no clues on that handsome face.

"I suppose I should have asked." I didn't, because unless it's some bottom of the barrel swill, I can appreciate almost any bourbon.

The bartender starts to say something, but Jake raises a hand to stop him. "Take a taste of mine."

My expression must relay my concerns about sipping from his glass. It's almost too friendly, not to mention hygiene and all that.

He leans in and whispers right below my temple, only for my ears, "Can't catch the clap from sharing whiskey. Alcohol kills all the germs."

His breath is hot against my scalp, and I feel the rush between my legs.

"In that case, maybe I should taste it first." My voice is low and breathy, and my concerns are no longer an issue. *Hygiene be damned.* I let him bring the glass to my lips, and I take a sip.

Both men watch me swirl the bourbon in my mouth, before swallowing and taking another sip. Jake is riveted.

"It's oaky. Very oaky. And very delicious." I glance at the bartender. I don't need to check to see if I'm correct about what's in the glass. I'm certain of it. "I'll have the Woodford Double Oak."

The bartender chuckles, and Jake whistles softly beside me.

"But since it's not anywhere near five o'clock yet, I'll have mine over ice—a big cube."

The bartender nods. "A twist?"

"Orange, please."

"You know bourbon," Jake murmurs, his gaze shrewd and intense.

For a moment, I catch a glimpse of the intense man from the other night, but before I take a single breath he's gone, and charming Jake is back. Maybe I'm reading too much into the intensity. Maybe I'm looking for any excuse to say *no*.

"I like a woman who knows what she wants," he continues, "and isn't afraid to ask for it."

"The other day you said you like women who are trouble-makers. I'm beginning to think you just like women. Period."

"Isn't that the truth." He shakes his head. "Although I like some more than others."

The bartender brings a small silver bowl of caramel corn with my drink. It's their signature bar snack, but I can't eat it. Although, I should put something in my stomach.

"If I'm going to day drink, I need to eat something. Have you had lunch?"

"Nothing solid." Jake turns to the bartender. "Got a menu?"

He nods and pulls two cards from under the bar and hands them to us. The choices are limited which makes it easy.

"I'll have the house salad with roast chicken, please."

"And I'll have the burger," Jake replies. "Medium rare."

The bartender nods. "What kind of fries?"

Jake turns to me, before answering. "You are going to help me eat them, right?"

Definitely. I shrug. "Probably."

"Then tell the man what kind of fries you like."

"You don't have a preference?"

He shakes his head.

"Sweet potato. With some extra ketchup, please," I add, handing back the menu.

Since I can't charge anything to my room, I take out my credit card to start a tab.

Jake scowls at the card. "What are you doing with that thing?"

"You bought the drinks. I'm the one who suggested lunch. My turn to buy."

He swivels my stool to face him. "Put the damn plastic back in your wallet and don't pull it out again while you're with me." His tone is even, but firm enough that I don't bother to argue.

"I realize you were raised by a good Southern woman, but I can't let you buy me drinks *and* lunch." *You're not going to buy your way into my bed.* "It doesn't seem right."

"Why not? You're good company." He lifts his glass and holds my gaze steady. "To unexpected pleasures."

His eyes are dark like sin, and I'm quite sure the pleasure he's talking about is the salacious kind. Just the thought of it makes my flesh tingle *everywhere*.

Ari's right. Every man who sees my breasts doesn't need to be relationship material. I need to start looking at men as strictly fun.

Although I'm not sure Jake would be fun. Even when he's in a light mood, fun seems too breezy of a word to describe anything he might offer. Cling to the sheets, white-hot bliss—yes, that's more like it.

I touch my glass to his. "To unexpected pleasures."

"May the day be filled with them," he murmurs, his voice like coarse gravel.

When he takes a drink, his throat ripples, sending zings of electric current through me.

Maybe a night in his bed would be amazing. *I'm a good person and I deserve a little amazing.* I sneak a peek at him from the corner of my eye.

There's no maybe about it. It would be amazing. He exudes a raw sexuality that I've never seen up close and personal.

Even though a part of me knows he's the devil in sheep's clothing—*a damn sexy devil*—I give him my best *I'll have sex with you* smile—one that would make Ariana proud.

If he wants some unexpected *pleasure*, I'm all in.

12

JAKE

By the time we've put a dent in the food, sex is inevitable. From the way she flushes when I *accidentally* brush against her, she must sense it too.

From the beginning, I cranked up the charm several notches, and I'm doing everything in my power to make her feel safe. If this is going to work, she needs to trust me enough to go to my room, take off her clothes, and grant me permission to—do as I please.

I want her consent. I want her to *beg* me to defile her. I want there to be no doubt in her mind that she was a willing participant in her ruin.

Yes, I could overpower her—easily. But the aftermath will be earth-shattering—for all of them—if she's an eager partner. It'll be more satisfying for me, too.

I'm completely in control. I don't dwell on who she is—or who she belongs to. I don't allow myself to think about the past or to jump to the end game. I'm focused on the here and now—on her, like she's my sole reason for living.

I'm a pro at compartmentalizing. Everything packed away in its own bin. Her bin is labeled *Justice for Willow*.

Problems only occur when the bin becomes too full, or if I shove something inside that's especially volatile. If it explodes, it dirties everyone and everything for miles and miles. *It's a risk I'm willing to take today.*

I just hope like hell I can continue to hold it all together. The last thing I need is to slit her throat while she comes around my cock. Ford would be pissed if I called him to clean up that mess.

"Are you married?" Madeline asks, between bites of romaine.

I snicker. "Noooo. Why do you ask?"

She lifts a shoulder. "Ford promised to send the picture from the other night, but he hasn't. We wondered if maybe there was a wife or girlfriend somewhere and you guys didn't want to get caught in a bar with girls."

She's decided to let me fuck her. She's just checking the boxes, now.

"No woman anywhere. Not me, or Ford for that matter. I'll tell him your friend's still waiting on the picture." *I'm sure he'll jump right on it.*

"What about you? You got some guy back home waitin' on you?"

"No guy back home." She stills, searching my face, her eyes wary. "Would it matter?"

"Matter to me?" I run my knuckles down her cheek. Her skin is warm and silky, and her expression open and honest. *Pure and innocent.* It almost veers me off course. *Almost, but not quite.*

"Not to me. Not at this point, pretty girl. You're much too tempting. But I hope it would matter to you."

She lifts her head high. "It would."

I believe her. She doesn't take after her father, who never met a pussy he didn't want to stick his dick into. *But she has his genes.*

"You're doing a lousy job of helping me with these fries," I tease, stepping back into role to distract me from her flawless skin and doe eyes—her innocence. "Not letting you back out now."

I drag a fry through the ketchup and bring it to her lips. She takes a bite, and I use my thumb to wipe a bit of ketchup from the edge of her mouth before she can lick it away.

When I touch her, she blushes a beautiful shade of red that rouses something inside me. If I put a finger to her throat, I'd feel a pulse thrumming hard and fast.

I pick up another fry, dip the end in ketchup, and bring it to her mouth—stopping inches from those glistening lips. My cock is restless as I hold her gaze. "Open for me, nice and wide."

Her eyes grow more dilated as she presses her legs together and squirms on the barstool.

Oh Scarlet, you're going to be so much fun to break.

Slowly, I bring the fry closer, pulling it back when she shifts to reach it. "Let me feed you," I murmur. "Can you wait patiently, like a good girl?"

She gazes up at me through thick, dark lashes and nods, and I feel her submission deep in my balls.

After a moment passes, I allow her to take a bite, but not before I place a drop of ketchup on her bottom lip. This time, instead of my thumb, I use my tongue to lap it up.

I couldn't care less that we're in public, and right now, I suspect she doesn't care, either.

A small moan escapes her, and I slide a hand through her long, dark hair, cup that gorgeous face, and press my mouth to hers.

Her lips are plump and smooth, *inviting*, even warmer than her skin. My mouth is gentle, but firm. As the seconds tick by, the kiss becomes rougher, demanding and like the good girl she promised to be, she's patient and takes what I give. *Oh, baby, you are too perfect.*

When my thoughts and emotions begin to tangle, I pull my mouth away and give myself some time to get back on track.

Her mouth is open slightly, and her neck is the same shade of red as her knit dress. *Such an alluring shade of red.* None of this is making it easy to keep myself in check.

"I want you, Madeline. I want to do sweet things to you," I touch my forehead to hers, "and I want to do dirty things to you. I think you want that too."

She swallows hard. "I've never—you're a stranger."

I expected this. She's not giving off virgin vibes, but she's not terribly experienced. She needs a little push. *She needs permission.*

I pull my head back slightly so she can look into my eyes, and I take her fingers between mine. "We're not exactly strangers, are we?"

She tips her head to the side. "Is Jake your real name?"

She needs more reassurance. That I can give her. "Jacob is my legal name. But most everyone calls me Jake."

She nods, and I give her a moment before I nudge. "One night, pretty girl. No strings—just fun. Lots of fun."

"Fun," she whispers.

"Haven't you ever wanted to live out a fantasy?"

She doesn't say a word, but I see the wheels turning. *Almost there.*

"If it makes you feel safer, I can leave my ID with the front desk. We can ask them to hold on to it until you give them permission to return it to me. That way you'll know exactly how to track me down."

I'm willing to hand over my driver's license, if that's what it takes. But it's not going to happen, because then the front desk clerk will know that she's hooking up with a man she doesn't know. Sheltered women are willing to take risks to avoid embarrassment. They don't know a world where bad things happen to them.

Her breath is a series of short, choppy spurts when she places her hands on my thighs. "I want to be with you. But before we—I should tell you—I lied. My name's not Madeline."

The last thing I want is her honesty, although it's a sweet confession. I place two fingers to her lips before she can say more. "Don't tell me your name. You haven't done this before. There's something freeing about anonymity, Scarlet."

Her brow furrows. "Scarlet?"

"From the moment I saw you, in the bar the other day, I thought of you as Scarlet. First, it was the sparkly red shirt. Then later, when you were uncomfortable, a beautiful shade of scarlet stained your cheeks."

She lowers her head. "Oh my God—you must think—"

I lift her chin with my fingers. "I think you're perfect."

I press a kiss to the bridge of her nose, and signal for the bartender. "A bottle of fifteen-year Elk's Crossing Reserve to go. Charge it to my room." He hedges, and I hand him a couple of fifties. "For your trouble."

"Why Elk's Crossing?" She tenses and studies my face carefully.

"When Ford ordered drinks the other night, he asked for the best bourbon in the house. The waitress brought Elk's Crossing Reserve. I don't see any reason you shouldn't have the best in the house too."

The lies glide off my tongue, one after another. But she nods and her features relax. That's all I care about right now.

"But tonight, no shots. We'll show it the respect it deserves."

She smiles softly, and her eyes glitter with arousal. "I have fantasized about hooking up with a stranger." She averts her eyes. "Who I met in a club. I just haven't had the courage to act on it."

I place a hand on either side of her head, nudging her beautiful face up until our mouths meet in a kiss filled with raw passion and wanton need—mine and hers. We devour each other until we're breathless, but I don't let go of her.

"Let me help you play out that fantasy. One night. You can be as naughty as you like. Just you and me until the sun comes up, and then we say goodbye and go back to our boring lives."

I press a small kiss to the tip of her nose. "You won't regret it. I promise." *Not tonight, anyway.*

13

JAKE

WHEN WE GET to the suite, I toss the keycard on the nearest flat surface and take the bourbon and an eager Scarlet to the bedroom. We've had our hands all over each other since the bar, and she doesn't protest.

She stops just inside the bedroom door to take off her boots. "The Christmas decorations in here are lovely."

Fucking Christmas everywhere.

I grunt. "Not anywhere near as lovely as you." I sink my teeth into the side of her neck and hold her hips steady, while she toes off the boots.

She shivers. "You're making this harder than it has to be."

"My specialty," I murmur, tightening my hold on her.

When she's finally barefoot, I lead her to an upholstered chair several feet from the bed.

Dragging her onto my lap, I glance at the top of the curtain rod where one of the cameras is lodged.

The blood pumps through my veins when I spot it, breathing life into every corner of my dark soul. Every cell is primed for success. I'm *that* close to justice.

Morality is never black and white—it's gray and murky.

Luring her into my game might not be right, but it's righteous. No one can convince me otherwise.

Scarlet shifts on my lap, raining kisses along my neck. My cock weeps for a taste of her. But I need to go slow—to arouse her beyond the point of no return, where she couldn't stop, even if she wanted to. *I'm too close for her to change her mind now.*

My thumb finds her nipple through the layers of fabric, coaxing it gently. When it peaks, I move to the other. All the while, my mouth is on her throat, whispering sweet nothings into the sensitive skin.

I lick her clavicle and gently blow on it. She trembles and purrs like a kitten. She's a heavenly sight. Sweet and comfortable in my arms—too comfortable.

Impatient to push her boundaries, I reach under her dress and slide my fingers along her inner thigh. The skin is velvety and I could play here for hours, but her pussy beckons—more enticing than the call of the Siren—and I won't deny myself.

Her heart pounds as I inch closer to her cunt. Not so different from how any animal reacts when a predator approaches. The body often senses demise, before the brain can alert us to run.

She smiles at me. A shy smile that *almost* lands in my chest.

"You're a beautiful woman, but when you're aroused, you're breathtaking."

She sweeps her hand over the stubble on my face and lets it rest near my heart. When I push aside her thong to explore, she digs her fingertips into my chest.

"You're so wet, Scarlet." I run my nose along her jaw. "Do you know how much that pleases me?"

She doesn't reply, and I brush some loose strands off her face. "Do you?"

"Yes," she whispers, and I reward her by stroking my thumb firmly over the swollen bud, leaving no part untouched.

I observe carefully, while she enjoys my fingers. I take note of every hitch of breath, every gasp, every time she squirms or cants her hips. If I'm going to own her, I want to know what makes her pussy tighten and throb. I want to know everything.

"Are you a good girl, Scarlet, or are you a pretty little slut?"

She tenses but doesn't utter a peep.

"Which do you prefer?"

Her eyelashes flutter but she keeps her eyes closed to avoid the shameful truth. "I—I don't know."

"I think you do. Tell me. Then I'll tell you what I think." I pause to relish her discomfort, but not long enough for the shame to get too noisy. *It's much too soon for that.*

"What we do this afternoon and tonight, what we say, stays between us. I won't judge you for what you like, and I know you won't judge me, either." *Although, when it gets out that you're a filthy whore who'll fuck anything to get off, others will judge you—harshly, I expect.*

"I'm not sure." She opens her eyes, and I see the embarrassment that often hinders inexperienced women from seeking pleasure on their terms. "A good girl, I—I guess."

I smooth her hair, enjoying the feel of it on my palm. "I think you like both. I think you want to be my good girl *and* my pretty little slut. That makes me so happy, Scarlet," I whisper against the ridge of her ear, my lips playing on the sensitive skin.

She whimpers, and her head bobs up and down. The movement is barely perceptible, but I see it.

With slow and meticulous strokes, I lavish attention on her pussy with one hand, and pet her all over—everywhere I can reach—with the other.

When her moans become desperate, I slide one finger, and then two, into her tight little cunt. She's drenched, but it's a snug fit. The kind of snug that makes my balls tighten—until my conscience bites.

This is wrong—blasphemous. I shouldn't enjoy pleasuring her so much. *She's the enemy,* my conscience screeches.

I shake off the feeling.

Scarlet trembles when I find the rough spot on her inner walls. I let her revel in the sensation, but as soon as she bucks, I pull my hand away.

She's confused and it makes my balls throb.

I run my tongue over my fingers, then bring them to her mouth.

"You taste like honey." It kills me to admit it, but it's the truth. I should hate this. I should despise her taste, but I don't. My insides wither at the realization—but not my cock.

"Taste how sweet you are when you want me."

She opens her mouth, round and wide, and all I want is to shove my dick through that O.

She's a job, a dirty job that you need to do. It doesn't matter how your body reacts. It's what's in your soul that matters.

My fingers settle between her legs again, and she moans as they quicken. It's a beautiful sound, shaky and deep, and it leaves my dick jonesing to destroy her cunt.

Not yet.

"Let's have a drink." I slide a hand from under her dress, and she pouts, like a woman who's not turning back. "Don't worry, darlin'. I'm going to give you everything you need."

I open the bottle, pulling off all the sharp foil before handing it to her. "Take a sip."

She eyes the elk on the bottle, while I bring it to her lips, but doesn't comment.

When she's had enough, I take a swig of the poison, reminding myself that my sister died because of this swill. *I know that's why it happened. I've always known it, and someone will pay for her death. I've always known that too.*

I replace the cap securely, appreciating the long, curved

bottleneck, characteristic of the brand. "I'm going to rock your world, Scarlet, but I need something from you too."

She tilts her head, touching my face. For a moment, I allow myself to enjoy her touch, knowing I'm a traitor for it. I don't push her fingers away until the smell of burnt flesh fills my nostrils.

I need to get control of my body—my emotions.

I take a deep breath, yank up the fabric of her dress until her pussy is within easy reach, and slowly, I rub her clit.

When my thumb slides below the fleshy hood, I'm rewarded with gasps and little cries. She clings to me, and my mouth curls.

"I need you to trust me—to follow my instructions. Can you do that?"

14

MADELINE

"WHAT KIND OF INSTRUCTIONS?" I'm not sure why I bother asking. I'm *desperately* aroused. If he *instructed* me to hump the stuffed Santa on the armoire, I would. No questions asked.

Everything about this, about him, is filthy—and amazing. Mind-blowing. I don't know if I'd ever do anything like this again, but my God, I don't want to stop—I don't want him to stop.

"Close your eyes," he demands, and when I do, he slides his fingers into my pussy. I mewl as my walls pulse around them.

"Rock your hips into my hand." His voice is like butter, and I follow his commands like they're gospel. "That's a good girl," he murmurs, and every inch of me blooms under his praise. "Just like that."

When I was a child, I loved the verbal stroking from pleasing the teacher. Apparently, I still love it, only now instead of feeling it in my chest, I feel it in my pussy.

"Tell me how you feel."

Like I'm floating above the clouds, on my way to heaven. "It's incredible—you're incredible."

"Open your eyes, Scarlet."

I open them immediately. It's late afternoon and the room is dim, but my eyes adjust quickly. The fading light casts a dark shadow over his face, but he's beautiful, nonetheless. I stroke his cheek—I can't resist.

"Those are the kind of instructions I'm talkin' about. You did perfectly."

Instead of being embarrassed that I'm in a stranger's bed, mindlessly following directions as he leads me astray, my heart swells with pride.

"Was it hard?"

I shake my head. "It was easy." *Too easy.* Where will he draw the line? *Where will I?*

"Easy," he murmurs. The navy flecks in his eyes shimmer, and I can see how much I've pleased him.

I nod, and he takes a small section of my hair and rubs it reverently between his fingers, like it's made of spun silk anointed by the Almighty.

"When you obey and submit to my will, it allows me to give you pleasure, which gives me pleasure."

I want pleasure. And I want to give him pleasure too.

There's something heady about pleasuring him—of playing on the same field as someone who is so self-assured, so confident, so powerful. I can't explain it.

He lets my hair slide through his fingers. "You ready to submit a bit more?"

I nod enthusiastically. *I love this game—maybe too much.*

One side of his mouth curls, and I see the dimple that makes him seem human—like the rest of us.

"Go over and stand by that chair." He points to a padded rocker across from the windows.

I climb off him and saunter over to the chair like I haven't got anything in the world to tend to but him.

"Take off your pretty dress for me."

My insides quiver. I'm willing to have sex with him in any

position he wants. Taking off my clothes while he watches—
takes stock of my body—is difficult. Maybe too difficult. It
doesn't matter how I actually look—in my head, I'm the fat girl.

I stare at my feet. *What if I can't do this? Will he be disappointed? It doesn't matter. I'll be disappointed enough for us both.*

"Scarlet, look at me."

I lift my head, but I'm so shaken inside, I don't really
see him.

"Don't close your eyes, and don't avert your gaze until I give
you permission. Even if it gets uncomfortable—especially if it
gets uncomfortable. I'll help you through it. Do you
understand?"

I nod, even though I want to crawl under the covers with
him and shed my clothes there.

"Take off your clothes. I want to see the lingerie you picked
out this morning."

I take a long breath, and slowly untie my wrap dress. My
hands are shaking, and his eyes are dark as he watches, but
even in the low light they sparkle. *What if he doesn't like what he
sees?*

As I fumble with a delicate snap, I catch the outline of his
hard cock through his trousers. *He wants you. You did that to
him. He wants you.*

The realization lifts the weight off my shoulders and spurs
me on.

I let my dress fall to the floor and step out of it, wearing
nothing but a pure white bra edged in lace and matching
thong. My cheeks are warm, but a small smile plays on my lips.
I wonder if he likes his good girls in virginal white?

His breath hitches as he regards me, and my body confidence shoots to the moon.

"Oh Scarlet, you are *so* perfect. Come here."

I don't hesitate to go to him.

As I approach, I see some of the intensity from the other

night. But it doesn't frighten me today. It looks like lust. Pure, unfettered, *I'm going to fuck you so hard you won't walk for a week* lust that makes my knees weak.

He stands and dips his head, nibbling on my neck as he unclasps my bra.

When my breasts bounce free, he palms them, rolling a nipple in each hand until I'm swaying toward his cock.

"When I play with your tits, do you feel it in your cunt?"

He says it so softly, so sweetly, that it takes a moment before I realize the words are dirty—like him. *Like me.*

I tighten my arms around him, aching to feel every muscle under my fingertips while he devours my mouth and hooks his thumbs into my thong. Using the delicate fabric, he yanks me closer. I feel the pull and then the tear. When he drags his mouth away, the lace is in a small pile at my feet.

Every move he makes takes us one step closer to sex. It's an erotic dance—wherever he leads, I follow.

"Sit in the rocking chair," he commands, "and hook your legs over the arms so I can see your pussy glisten."

I gasp audibly, but I do it—not just to please him, but to please myself.

When I'm seated, the rough fabric prickles against my skin, but the sensation is fleeting as I lie back and spread my legs wide, completely open to him.

My skin feels hot and my mouth dry.

I'm naked and he's fully dressed as he lowers himself to his haunches and tongues my wet flesh. I gasp and wriggle at the first pass of his tongue.

"Stay still," he warns, licking me until I can't breathe.

"Do you like my mouth on you?" His voice is gravel. I hear the need.

"I love it," I pant, seconds from begging him to keep licking me.

He smirks, and I want nothing more than to grab him by the ears and drag his mouth back to my pussy.

"Before you can have my mouth again, I want you to touch yourself like you do when you're alone." He taps a finger on my clit and sits back on his heels. "I want to know what makes that pussy sing."

His eyes are black and his breathing ragged as he watches me slide my hands over my breasts, across my belly, to my pussy that's aching for attention. I'm nowhere near as embarrassed as I would expect. It's just me and him for one night.

I don't need to dip my fingers inside to find the moisture. I'm plenty wet.

Jake tips up my chin, and I fight the urge to hide. Instead, I gaze into his eyes and lick my lips while I play with myself.

I've never done this before—not with someone watching—but every wave of pleasure sends sparks skittering through me. *The orgasm is going to shatter me.* It's all I focus on while I swirl my fingers over the slick flesh, applying just the right pressure to make me come quickly.

His eyes are hooded, and his desire for me is palpable.

I am *so* close.

"My pretty little slut," he murmurs. "Such a good girl."

So close. His face seems faraway—fuzzy.

When I'm *almost* there, he swats my hand away, and I protest, until he replaces my fingers with his mouth. Relief blankets me, and I groan, aching for release.

The relief is short-lived. Jake is in no hurry as he eats me, avoiding my clit as I squirm shamelessly for something to rub against.

I'm about to scream when he pulls his mouth away. But there's something hard and cold between my legs. Startled, I shift on the seat and look down at my thighs.

He's sliding the long, curved neck of the Elk's Crossing

bottle over my pussy. The glass is icy against my hot flesh, but I'm panting uncontrollably.

"Shhh," he coos, holding me in place with a hand on my belly. "It's okay. You have a vibrator, don't you?"

"Yes. But—"

"It's no different."

But it is different—more complicated.

The glass glides back and forth over my swollen clit, and I hang onto the chair like my life depends on it.

I'm about to combust. It feels so damn good I don't care that it's my family's bourbon sloshing inside the bottle as it rolls across my pussy.

"You're almost there, pretty girl."

I am.

My belly tightens, and when I lift my hips to grind against the bottle, he slips the neck into my pussy.

Oh my God. "Jake!" I wail, but not because I want him to stop.

"Scarlet, you're beautiful, lying back, legs spread so nicely for me while I fuck you with this nice toy." He strokes my clit with his free hand, and my cries fill the air as I writhe.

"Feels good, doesn't it?"

I nod—at least I think I do.

"Say it, Scarlet…tell me how good it feels to be fucked like this."

"So good," I whimper, clinging to the arms of the chair.

"My pretty little slut is such a good, good girl," he coos.

Yes. I'm such a good girl.

"Do you want to watch me slide the bottle in and out of your cunt?"

Yes.

I peek between my legs and watch as the bottle neck disappears inside me. *Oh God.*

"You're making a mess all over the chair," he tuts, and I turn my head away and close my eyes. "You're almost ready to take my cock."

I want that—I want his cock, but I don't want him to stop what he's doing to give it to me.

"Let go, Scarlet." He increases the pressure on my clit, and I dig my fingers into the chair and buck wildly.

"Let go."

His fingers play me so expertly that I have no choice. My belly tightens almost painfully, and I tremble as I fall, gasping for air like I'm dying.

"That's it. So beautiful." He lets up on my clit for a moment, but the bottle is still wedged in me and my walls cling to it, as if to keep it inside.

"Your pussy is throbbing so hard. It needs more, Scarlet. Come for me, again."

No. It's not possible. "Can't." I whimper and thrash, but he places a hand on my belly, again, to hold me in place.

"You can. I'm going to make you come all night. We're just getting started."

15

JAKE

I IMAGINE her swollen cunt tightening and squeezing the glass bottle until it aches as much as my balls ache.

After she comes a second time, I ride her through the orgasm until she stops flailing and her cries are soft purrs that sound like victory.

I hold up the bottle. The graceful neck is opaque, coated with her juices.

She throws an arm over her eyes.

"Don't hide from me, Scarlet, and don't be embarrassed. We like what we like. No apologies."

Slowly, she moves her arm. Her face is flushed, and her eye makeup is smudged and pooled under her shining eyes. *Well-fucked and thoroughly ruined.* But I'm not done.

I scoop her up and carry her to the bench at the foot of the bed, the bourbon tucked under my arm. She clings to me, eyes closed. Her breathing is not yet normal. "You okay to stand?"

She nods. "Yes."

I place her on her feet and lower myself to the edge of the bench, facing her.

Her eyes are still a little unfocused. She smells of sex, and her hair is an untamed mass, with thick strands matted to her sweaty face. But even in ruins, she's gorgeous, and I want those plump, sweet lips around my cock.

"On your knees, Scarlet." My voice is gentle, cajoling, and I have no doubt she'll obey.

She's a little shaky, but with a bit of help, she eases to the rug and settles between my legs.

There's something about a Langford on her knees that brings the demons close to the surface. I don't bother to push them away. *Let them lurk.*

"Take out my cock, like a good girl." I'm struggling for control, and my voice has an edge to it now. But Scarlet doesn't blink. She unbuckles my belt and fumbles with the zipper, freeing my rock-hard cock.

Her mouth is slack, and I suck in a breath as my shaft thickens, inches from her face.

All I can think about is how sweet her cunt tastes, and how I want to feast on it again. *Traitor,* my conscience shouts. *Traitor!*

I pick up the damn bourbon and pour some into my cupped hand as she watches intently. I hold my breath and douse my cock with the amber spirit, like it's holy water.

"What are you doing?" she shouts. "It's going to burn!"

Burn, it does. I squeeze my eyes together and let my head fall back. It burns so good. *It's my punishment. My redemption.*

My cock is purple and angry, but it's still long and hard and I want to fuck her more than I want my next breath.

She reaches for a throw behind me and tries to wipe the bourbon off my skin. I grab it from her and toss it aside. I want the pain. I welcome it.

I palm my cock. "Lick it clean. Suck it into your throat, and then tell me if Elk's Crossing tastes as good on my cock as it does over ice."

Her mouth is open, and she looks aghast. I'm not sure what

she's going to do, until she wets her lips and draws me into that velvety mouth.

I gasp like a schoolboy. The burn of the alcohol and her hot, wet mouth are a deadly combination. I open myself to the pain, struggling as it begins to abate, but eventually I succumb, allowing my conscience to tear into me as the agony turns to bliss.

Without regard for her, I thrust harder, deeper, to satisfy the worst of my demons. But there's no satisfying them.

When I can't hold back a second longer, I hold her head between my hands and empty my cock into her throat.

She retches, and I smile, easing out of her mouth.

I'm not sure why I do it, but I pull her toward me, and she rests her head on my thigh.

"Why did you do that with the bourbon?" she murmurs. "Surely you knew it would burn."

"I did. But I also knew you'd make it feel better."

It's the truth, and I hate myself right now as much as I've ever hated anything. I can't tell the difference between delivering her ruin and satisfying my need for her.

I'm hard again, and even as she lies sweetly at my feet, I want to punish her. God help me, I want it in the worst way.

Without warning, I lift her off the floor and toss her on the bed.

"On all fours and wait quietly while I undress."

While I step out of my pants and retrieve a condom from my wallet, the garland draped around the mirror above the dresser catches my eye, and I yank it down and bring it to the bed.

I climb between her legs and let my hands roam her body, massaging and gentling until I feel her relax.

"I need you," I rasp. "I don't want to let you go until I've had a chance to be inside you. Let me have that."

I've lost all sight of what's truth and fiction. The lies are

17

NINETEEN YEARS EARLIER

Cain

THERE'S a handful of people milling around the courtroom. Not my mama, though. She ain't ever been around when I need her. Why should today be any different?

"Pay attention, Cain," my court-appointed lawyer, Mr. Dyson, chides while we wait for the judge.

I might be the one in trouble, but Dyson smells like he gargled some of Big Vern's hooch before he left the house this morning. Although, even sober, the guy doesn't seem all that smart, or maybe he doesn't give a damn about someone like me.

But what do I know?

I'm just a fifteen-year-old punk from Hagerstown, Kentucky, deep in coal mine country—or what's left of it. Hagerstown's only a few hours from here, but it's so different from St. Germaine it might as well be on the other side of the world.

"Remember to address the judge as 'sir' or 'Your Honor.' If you know what's good for you, you'll mind your manners."

Blah, blah, blah. Same shit he told me when we were in court last week.

"All that's required is that you respond to the judge's questions the way we talked about. You do that, and soon you'll be able to put this whole mess behind you."

I might feel better about following his advice if he bothered to look at me when he talked. Maybe not. None of what Dyson says makes a lick of sense, and I have no reason to trust this guy —not when my life's on the line.

I lean in so the prosecutor at the table beside us can't hear. "Even after sleepin' on it for a week, I still think it's a bad idea to admit to doin' something I didn't do."

"But you did do it," he replies, scribbling some words on a yellow notepad.

"I told you a hundred times. I broke into Langford's office and snooped in some desks and file cabinets. I made a mess, but I did not have a gun. Someone planted it in my rucksack. Probably one of the deputies."

"Hold on," he mutters when a tall woman with earrings shaped like Christmas ornaments calls the lawyers up to a table near where the judge sits.

I'm sure she has something nasty to say about me, and what I've done.

Can't change the past.

If only I'd thought long and hard about those words that night. Although it probably wouldn't have made any difference. That night, the past was all I had left.

It was my fifteenth birthday and there was no one alive who cared if I lived or died, and nothing to mark the day. I'm not talking about presents or a two-layer cake from the pink bakery downtown, just someone to wish me a happy birthday—someone who was glad I'd been born.

My sister Willow had always woken me up singing that silly birthday song. She couldn't carry a tune to save her life, but she made up for it by pouring her love into every note. We couldn't afford a cake, not even one made from a box, but she made sure I had my own cupcake every year—not a stale one they set aside for the pigs—with a mountain of real buttercream piped on top, and a blue candle with white stripes. I never knew where she got the money, but it cost her something. I'm sure of it.

She'd tell me to make a big wish before I blew out the candle. Every year, I wished for the same thing: that I'd grow up to be filthy rich so I could take care of Willow, the way she'd always taken care of me. I had big plans for us. Starting with Christmas.

I'd cut down a giant fir and tie it to the top of my big-ass truck. On Christmas Eve, we'd sit by a roaring fire near the tree and float marshmallows shaped like snowmen in hot chocolate made with fresh milk. There'd be two dozen cupcakes on a silver tray and sugar cookies shaped like the stars Willow was always wishing on.

Christmas morning, there'd be so many presents for my sister under the tree that we wouldn't be able to see the red velvet skirt wrapped around the base. It would be so magical that Willow would forget all about what it had been like to fight with the rats over scraps of leftover food before falling asleep, cold and hungry.

She was all I had in life, and I miss her so much it hurts. But the hole in my heart was especially big that night.

After dark, I went to the distillery. Someone set up a memorial with a stone bench near where the fire had happened, and I wanted to visit for a while.

I followed the smell of ashes and burnt flesh to the back of the Langford property. On my way, I passed the big white house with electric candles flickering in every window. Smoke bellowed from both chimneys, snaking its way into the cold air, and there was an enormous Christmas tree, all lit up, in the picture window, like the one I always wished for when I blew out my birthday candle. It was all real pretty, like something you'd see on TV, and I stopped for a minute to look.

That's when I saw her. The little Langford girl twirling around the tree like a sugar plum fairy.

It wasn't right that they were celebrating Christmas after their fire killed all those people. It wasn't fair that their girl was alive, and my sister was dead.

As I watched the girl dance in her warm house with white lights twinkling around her, anger coiled in my chest until it was tighter than a rattlesnake before the kill.

I couldn't see straight. Couldn't think straight, either. I needed justice for Willow, and I needed it more than my next breath.

"Where were we?" Dyson asks when he returns to his seat.

"I was sayin' that one of the deputies planted the gun."

"Keep your voice down," he hisses. "We've been over this."

Yup, but you won't listen to the truth. I'd like to wring his scrawny neck. *I have to make him listen or I'm going to be locked up until I turn eighteen.*

"We've talked about this, but—"

"There is no but. You already told the court, under oath, that you did it. Too late to change your mind now. We're just here today for the sentencing. The prosecutor offered you a good deal. If you stay out of trouble, you'll stay out of jail."

"I don't see how it's such a good deal if I have to go to that juvie place. They don't let you come and go, and I'll be stuck there for three years."

He finally looks at me, his bloodshot eyes focused on my face. "You're underage, so even if they dropped the charges, you'd have to go somewhere and that somewhere is a group home. You wouldn't be free to come and go there, either. It's essentially the same as a juvenile facility. It's impossible to find a foster home for a fifteen-year-old boy, especially one who's trouble. Admitting culpability and showing remorse is the best way you can help yourself."

"All rise," the clerk calls in a shrill voice that startles me.

Everyone stands as Judge Caldwell strides into the court-room and climbs onto his throne.

My heart pounds like a sumbitch while I watch him shuffle some papers before acknowledging us.

"Are there any matters that we need to discuss before we get to the sentencing?" he finally asks.

"A couple of housekeeping matters, Your Honor," the prose-cutor replies, and they start talking about restitution, remorse, my age, and the penal code. I don't understand most of it, but I keep my mouth shut. The judge seems like he's in a foul mood, and I don't want to cause any more problems for myself.

The deputy who brought me here today coughs. He's been standing against the wall since we got here, eyeing me like I'm dirt. When I sassed him yesterday, he told me that if I didn't smarten up, I was going to end up in the penitentiary, where I'd make some big hairy guy a fine bitch.

I acted like it was no skin off my back, but the truth is, it scared the shit out of me.

I've been in juvenile lockup for two weeks, and even though they say that it's not as bad as the penitentiary, I can't wait to get out.

I'm used to roaming the streets. Spending so much time in a little box is making me stir-crazy, although I'd rather be crazy than some guy's bitch.

The deputy wasn't lying. Everyone knows what happens to people in jail, especially teenagers. I can be meaner than a wild boar, but I'm not done with puberty yet, and I hear that in the penitentiary they like them young, without too much hair.

My stomach twists like I'm about to puke. I take a drink of water, but it doesn't stop the scary shit that keeps popping into my head.

The judge could lock me up forever and no one would even know. At least if I was back home, I'd have the boys and a few other people who would notice if I didn't come around.

"Mr. Thompson," the judge says, addressing me in a stern voice that sends a shiver up my spine. "The prosecutor has recommended that you be remanded to a juvenile facility until you reach the age of eighteen. I'm not bound by the government's recommendation, nor am I inclined to follow it."

I'm not sure what he means. I glance at my lawyer, but his eyes are on Judge Caldwell.

"Am I boring you, Mr. Thompson?"

Mr. Thompson. He's just mockin' me, but I hold my tongue. "No, sir."

"Then look at me when I'm talking to you, boy."

I train my eyes on his, my hands shaking as bad as my stomach.

"You committed a despicable act. Trespassing on private property with a gun and the intention of doing malice. There was a young child in that home. Unforgiveable," he sneers. "I have a boy about your age, although that's where the similarities end. But if he'd done what you did, he'd suffer my wrath just like you're going to suffer. That's how boys are made into men."

Bullshit. That's how poor boys are broken, not made. Rich boys never have to suffer. Even if his son killed a woman, he'd walk away scot-free. The judge would see to it. That's how life works.

"One day you'll thank me for this."

I doubt it.

The judge nods at the deputy, who comes to stand behind me, so close I can hear him wheeze. It's chilly in here, but I'm sweating like a pig.

"Do you have anything to say for yourself, before I issue the sentence?"

I have plenty to say, but I better keep it short and contrite like Dyson told me.

"I didn't mean no one harm," I say sincerely. "I'm sorry for what I done." *Not so much.* "That gun wasn't mine, sir."

As soon as the last words are out of my mouth, I feel all eyes in the courtroom on me. I shouldn't have said the part about the gun, because it sounds like I'm making excuses, but I had to.

The judge shakes his head. "If I had a nickel for every time someone stood where you are, telling me that the gun that the sheriff's deputies found didn't belong to them, I'd be a rich man."

He pushes his glasses up on his nose and folds his hands in front of him, looking down on me. I feel like one of those Lego boys that the teacher tossed in the trash at the end of kindergarten, small and broken, that nobody's got any more use for.

"I don't think you are sorry, Mr. Thompson," the judge says, calling me a liar to my face, again. "I think what you are is a menace to society. Given half a chance, you'd have used that gun on the Langfords that night—innocent people. If it hadn't been for security, you'd have gunned them down in their home days before Christmas."

His face is hard and he's fighting mad. *I'm screwed.* I've always been screwed from the moment I came out of the womb. It's my fate.

"This court sentences you to two years for trespassing, three years for malicious destruction of property, five years for breaking and entering, fifteen years for possession of a handgun in the commission of a crime for a total of three counts, to be served consecutively. You are immediately remanded to the state penitentiary."

It takes a second to register. A second before I feel like I'm drowning. *You're going to make some big hairy guy a fine bitch.*

"No!" I shout. "We had a deal. I want a trial."

"Control your client, Mr. Dyson, or I'll tack on a contempt of court charge, and he'll spend a few more years behind bars."

When the last word is out of his mouth, he gets up and gathers some folders. "This matter is adjourned."

"All rise," the clerk cries as the judge leaves the courtroom.

I get right up in Dyson's face. "You told me that I would be sent to juvie for three years. This isn't right. You gotta do something. I don't want to go to the penitentiary."

"I'm as surprised as you," the bastard replies, shoving paperwork into his briefcase.

"Let's go." The deputy takes my arm roughly, but I shrug him off.

"Can't you do something?" I beg the lawyer. But before he answers, the deputy grabs me by the scruff of the neck, like I'm a dog who shit in the middle of the kitchen, and his buddy cuffs me.

"I'll meet you in lockup," Dyson mumbles as I'm being hauled off.

When I glance at the lawyer over my shoulder, I notice Langford—the lone spectator in the back of the courtroom. The fucker smirks at me like he just won the fuckin' lottery.

I want to ruin him, take his little girl from him like he took Willow from me. I want to beat him until there's blood all over his fancy suit—until there's not a breath left in his body. I killed a man once, and I'm not afraid to do it again.

"I ain't gonna be gone forever," I yell, glaring straight at the sumbitch, "and when I get out, I'm comin' for you."

THANK you for reading Carnal Vengeance. I hope you loved it! For more of Jake (Cain) and Scarlet read **Tainted King**, **https://amzn.to/3y1WYFh**

DEPRAVED EXCERPT

Chapter 1

GABRIELLE

"Ughhhh!" I whack the edge of the frozen laptop. "Why won't you behave tonight?"

"Can't beat those things into submission. I've tried."

An ominous chill raises gooseflesh, as I struggle to make sense of the voice. *It can't be. It just can't be.*

Can it?

Curling my fingers into the leather blotter, I lift only my eyes, peeking carefully over my lashes. A tremor builds as the animal filling my doorway comes into focus. Long and lean, a broad shoulder braced against the wooden frame, his right hand buried deep in the trouser pocket of a trim navy suit.

My heart bangs furiously on my chest wall, as though fighting to escape. Like the rest of me, it wants to run and hide.

But this is *my* office. *My* hotel. And I will not be cowed by JD Wilder.

Ever again.

I try to summon some anger so my voice won't wobble. My lips part to speak, but my mouth is dry, my tongue rough and heavy, and the words don't come.

"The hotel is stunning," he drawls, in that seductive baritone he uses to charm and cajole. "The photo layout in *Charleston Monthly* doesn't do it justice. You've done a hell of a job with the restoration."

His tone rankles me. Arrogant? Condescending? I'm not sure. But the annoyance stiffens my backbone, and allows the words to flow freely.

"How did you get in here?"

He says nothing.

"I'm sure you didn't come by after all these years to admire the hotel. Especially tonight. I'm surprised you're not at Wildwood Plantation, celebrating. Or commiserating."

With two long strides, he eats up the space between us, bringing the dark, musky scent of sin with him. When I dare to blink, my eyes flit to the starched white collar grazing his neck. It makes a sharp contrast to a jaw that hasn't seen a razor in days.

We peer at each other across the desk. It's awkward and uncomfortable. And dammit, my heart hurts. Just a little.

"It's been too long," he murmurs.

I lower my eyes to ease the discomfort, but his hands are there. Large and forbidding, splayed on my desk with both thumbs hooked under the carved lip. Skillful hands that probed and teased, wakening my flesh with a practiced touch. Luring me into dark, dreamy corners where there was only pleasure—until there wasn't.

I look away, my eyes searching desperately for a place to land. Somewhere safe that won't dredge up painful memories.

But there's no eluding him. No escaping the flood of emotion that took hold of me when he entered the room.

When I glance up, his jaw is set and his eyes dilated, as though they haven't grown accustomed to the dim light in the room. Or maybe he's remembering the white-hot nights, too.

The heat creeps up my neck, and I push the salacious thoughts away, focusing instead on how out of place his callused fingers look against the polished mahogany. But there is little reprieve for me.

"Gabrielle." My name glides off his tongue, as though he speaks it all too often.

I don't give him the satisfaction of looking up. I will not do it. He had my rapt attention once, and I'll be damned if he gets it again. Without even a cursory glance in his direction, I lift the stack of papers in front of me and bounce the edges off the desktop, again and again, until I'm satisfied each sheet has fallen into line.

"I have a business proposition for you."

A business proposition? After all this time? I don't buy it. Not for a single second. "I'm not interested."

"You will be."

"Not a chance."

How did he get in here? Georgina locked the door to the suite when she left for the day. I heard the lock catch. I know I did. "I'm still wondering how you obtained access to a private area in my hotel. Breaking and entering might be business as usual for you, but security is no small matter for me."

He steps back and lowers himself into a chair directly in front of the desk. The rich wool fabric stretches taut over his thighs, hugging the thick muscle like a second skin. I feel a small unwelcome pang between my legs. The barest of sensations. But *God help me,* it's there.

For a fleeting moment, I consider calling security. I want him gone, right now, before—

"Hear me out."

"You can't possibly have time for this tonight." I roll back the chair and stand to signal the discussion is over, but he doesn't budge, not even when I start around the desk to see him out. Anyone else would take the hint. But not JD. Yes, he knows I want him to leave. He just doesn't give a damn.

"I need you to go."

He doesn't blink, but his eyes travel over me in an all-too-familiar manner, before settling on mine. His gaze is steely. I suppose it's meant to make me heel. If so, he'll be disappointed. I'm not the love-struck teenager he coaxed into doing *anything* and *everything* he wanted. She's long gone.

"It wasn't a suggestion, Gabrielle. I might have phrased it politely, leaving you to believe there's a choice other than to listen, but it's not at all what I meant. You *will* hear me out. Sit."

Sit? The hell I will. "I am not a dog. And I prefer to stand, thank you."

"*Sit* down."

I'm torn. There's a small part of me that's curious, and a larger, saner part that wants to throw him out of my office before he utters another word. But above all else, what I want is to lash out and defy him. I want it with every living, breathing cell in my body.

But I don't kid myself. What I want is of no consequence. I've known JD my entire life, and he's not going anywhere until he has said everything he came to say.

I edge my backside onto the corner of the desk—*surely this qualifies as sitting*—and pull back my shoulders with my head high and proud. Only the fingers twisting in my lap hint at how anxious this man makes me.

"I'm sitting. Get on with it."

He says nothing.

JD plays a wretched little game when he wants the upper hand—which is pretty much all the time. He doesn't talk. He just observes and listens with the utmost patience, absorbing every nuance, every stutter, every tic of his victim's unease. He's cool and calculating, like a chess master, or a predator preparing to swoop in for the kill. When he decides you've suffered enough, he speaks carefully. It's mesmerizing to watch, unless you're the one caught in the cross hairs. I witnessed it dozens of times when we were younger, but even so, it's my undoing now.

He runs a thumb across his full bottom lip, arching a single disapproving brow at me.

I don't care. The extra height gives me confidence and helps me feel in control. But it's an illusion. And I know it.

"Your father took a loan from me. A loan he'll never be able to pay back."

"*What?*"

He might as well have said Martians landed on the Flag Tower at the Citadel, and they're occupying downtown Charleston as we speak. The idea of my father accepting a loan from him is *that* preposterous. "I-I-I don't believe you."

He says nothing.

How could my parents go to *him* without first talking to me? They weren't privy to any of the ugly details, but they know he hurt me. Yet, they went behind my back, told *him* things they kept from me, and took *his* money without a single word about it?

I struggle for composure, trying to make sense of why my parents would possibly go to him for money. I can't come up with a single thing.

I glance at him. He's watching from the catbird seat, waiting patiently for me to make a wrong move, say the wrong thing, so he can pounce. I imagine him backing me into a corner, swatting with his oversized paws like a big tomcat, toying with me until his hunger consumes him. Then devouring me in a single bite.

Gabrielle, get a grip. Do not let him do this to you.

I take a few calming breaths.

"My mother's very sick." It's the only reason I can come up with, but it doesn't make much sense. "If they needed money, they would have come to me." *Yes, of course they would have come to me before going to JD.* "I can't imagine why they'd go to you without talking to me first."

"And what would you be able to offer them?"

You smug bastard. "I own the hotel. I—"

"Oh stop. You don't have a prayer of coming up with the kind of money they need. You took every cent of equity out of this place to renovate and get it open. You're in debt over your head."

"You don't know a damn thing about me or my hotel."

"I know everything I care to know."

His voice is low and gruff, the sound achingly familiar. A small tug at the base of my belly fuels the anger and confusion.

"What do you want?"

JD leans back with an elbow draped casually over an arm of the chair. He deliberately brushes a piece of lint from his trousers before answering, as though even the most inconse-quential matters are more important than responding to me. "I'll get to that soon. First, let me fill you in on what's happening with your mother."

"What do you mean, *fill me in* on what's happening with my mother? What's going on with my mother?" *Lower your voice, Gabrielle. The hotel's filled with guests.* But right now, all I really care about is my mother.

"She's in good hands. Your parents left the city last night to get a second opinion about your mother's illness."

"They said they were going to the beach for a few days to spend some time alone before she begins treatment." Anger. Betrayal. Fear. Swirling and twisting until they're indistinguish-

able. "She already had a second opinion. Two additional opin-
ions," I choke out.

A lump gathers in my throat as I remember those appoint-
ments. How the doctors explained everything in excruciating
detail. Painting a vivid picture of the disease and how it would
progress. It was sobering—for me, for my mother—but especially for my father, who would do anything to change the
course for her. *Anything.* Including making a deal with the
devil, it appears.

"She had an appointment with a world-renowned immu-
nologist today. He's running some tests and is likely to confirm
the diagnosis, but he might have a more promising treatment to
offer that'll give her more good years."

"Where are they?" And why didn't they tell me any of this?

"It's up to them to tell you where they are. They don't want
to give you false hope in case the long-term prognosis doesn't
change. Your mother insists on keeping you in the dark until
they have more information."

I swallow my pride, and like a big, tasteless wad of chewing
gum, it catches at the back of my throat going down. My
parents are still keeping vital information from me as though
I'm a child. It never changes. "They don't want me to know
about any of it. Yet here you are."

"I have it on good authority the appointment went better
than expected."

"So much for privacy laws."

The smallest of smiles plays on his lips, but his eyes don't
twinkle. "Your mother will talk to you when she's ready."

"She'll talk to me now." I reach over and grab my cell phone
off the desk and call my parents, but it doesn't go through. I text
them, but the messages aren't delivered.

"You won't be able to reach them, Gabrielle."

"I don't care how powerful you think you are, even the president himself doesn't control the damn cellular network." My

voice is full of bravado, but in my heart, I know there's very little the Wilders don't control. Especially now, with DW a presidential candidate.

I lean over the desk, pick up the landline, and dial my parents' number from memory. I still can't get through. Panic begins to fill my chest, squeezing and tightening until it's difficult to breathe.

"Don't underestimate me, or my reach. There's no end to what I can make happen if it suits me."

A myriad of emotions roll through me, breaching the dam I painstakingly built in the last fifteen years. Pushing and pushing against the walls until there is nothing standing between visceral emotion and him. "I hate you."

My voice is raw with the hurt and betrayal he's dredged up. I don't want him to see the vulnerability, but I can't stop myself. "It wasn't enough to break my heart, to humiliate me and rub my nose in it. *No.* You won't be satisfied until you've taken everything."

Pain flashes in his eyes like a bolt of lightning slicing through a dark, empty canvas. I see it. It's there for just a brief second and then it's gone. But I'm certain it was there.

He's a heartless bastard and you are a fool, Gabrielle.

He crosses one leg over the other, an ankle resting on a knee. "Your parents can't afford the treatment." The tip of a long finger traces the inner seam of his shoe, gliding through the ridge where the soft cordovan leather meets the sole. "It's considered experimental even though they've had some success with it. Insurance won't cover any of it."

"When did you get to be such an expert on a rare autoimmune disease? And exactly why did you lend them money?"

"Before I agreed to pay for the cost of your mother's treatment, along with all their living expenses while they're away, I did some research. I don't throw around money idly."

He's calm, and I'm feeling just short of hysterical. I want to shake him. "*Why?* Why did you agree to help? What could you possibly want from them?"

He doesn't speak for at least a full minute, maybe more. It feels like hours slip away while we stare at each other. With each passing second, the silence grows louder until it shrieks like a banshee heralding my demise. This will not end well for me. I can feel it in my marrow, and the wait is excruciating. "What do you want?"

He doesn't answer right away, but when he does, it sucks all the oxygen from the room.

"You. I want you."

I wait for the punch line. Maybe a cruel laugh, and him to tell me I'm not fit to carry his trash to the curb. And I wait. Surely, I misunderstood. But one look at his stony face and I know there's no misunderstanding.

"*Me?*"

His gaze is penetrating. "I say what I mean, and I mean what I say. Always have. Nothing's changed."

Maybe he's not talking about sex. Maybe I've let my mind run away. Maybe he wants to use the hotel for some half-cocked scheme. Maybe. Maybe. Maybe.

"What do you want from me?"

"Whatever itch I need scratched."

Whatever itch I need scratched. Sex. He wants me to be his plaything. His whore.

My knees tremble until they can no longer support my weight. I grip the edge of the desk, and slump into the chair beside him. I'm done. It's been a long, trying day, and he's beaten what little fight I had left right out of me. I can't bear to hear any more from him. From the man who once professed his love for me. From the man who promised to protect me from all the evil in the world.

The room whirls, and a sour taste tickles my throat. My face is damp and clammy, and I can't decide if I'm going to vomit or faint first. Gripping the sides of my knees, I lower my head between my legs to stop the spinning.

He curses, and I hear the echo of my name and the faint rustle of his trousers, but it all seems so far away. I don't know how long I'm hunched over before he crouches next to me and pulls back my hair with a long, gentle sweep. "Take small sips," he instructs, wrapping my fingers around a paper cup.

I sit up slowly and do as instructed. Small sips until the nausea subsides and the room stills again. JD sits beside me, his chair angled toward me, assessing quietly while I pull myself together.

"Do you need to lie down?"

I shake my head and swallow the last drops of cool water, staring into the empty cup as though I might find some wisdom there.

"You want me? For—sex? You can't. Can't possibly. After all these years, why me?" I'm rambling. Barely managing choppy fragments between the short pants. My mind can't process any of this. Or it won't.

"It means exactly what you think it means."

I look up at him. He's tapping his fingers on the arm of the chair, his gaze devoid of any compassion. I search frantically, but can't find a single shred of decency anywhere in his face.

"But why me, JD?" My voice is louder now. Stronger. My thoughts more coherent. "Of all the women in Charleston. Of all the women who stalk your every move like you're a goddamn rock star. Why does it have to be me?"

He slides his wrist along the chair arm, as though he's polishing a scuff from the exposed wood. "Opportunity. Never been one to pass up a good opportunity, especially when it falls into my lap." His icy eyes meet mine. "Maybe I want something familiar. Or maybe I like the challenge. Take your pick."

He's not joking.

I'm stuck in his trap. Snared without a single hope of

freeing myself. My pulse pounds loudly in the silence while I search for an escape. "I'm engaged," I plead. It's a lie, but I'm desperate.

"*Pfft.* Engaged. Don't go there. Just don't."

I start to argue it's true, but I don't bother. It won't take much for JD to figure out that Dean and I broke up. Gossip travels through Charleston like a tiny hamlet. In a matter of days, everyone will know.

There's no way my father would have agreed to terms remotely like this. He would never do that to me. But JD is manipulative and cunning, and I wouldn't be shocked if he managed to trick my parents. I grip my seat and push out the words. Mentally preparing myself to be ripped apart. "My father agreed to this?"

Please say no. Please. I fill my lungs and hold the breath while waiting for an answer.

He looks aghast. "Don't be ridiculous."

I slowly release the breath, and relax my hold on the chair. "Then why are you here?"

"I'm not interested in his money."

"This has nothing to do with me. It's between you and him."

"Not anymore."

"What if I don't—agree to your terms?"

"I turn off the tap, and your mother doesn't get access to the beneficial treatment."

My hand instinctively flies to my mouth to cover a gasp. Of all the terrible things he's said today, this stuns me most. "Even you wouldn't be that spiteful. Not to my mother. You wouldn't."

"Don't underestimate me." He sits back in the chair, lifts his chin, and stares straight into my eyes. "I would hate to see her suffer. Your parents worked for my family for a long time. As far back as I can remember. They were always good to us, especially after the accident. But business is business."

Chapter 2

GABRIELLE

BUSINESS IS BUSINESS? His cruelty re-energizes me.

"Is that what you think? Is that how you think about life? About relationships? It's all transactional? God help you."

"I've never been a fool who turns to God for help."

No, JD doesn't believe in God. Not after his mother died. Praying to God is for the rest of us foolish mortals. I tuck a loose curl behind my ear, plotting a way forward. "How much does he owe you?"

"After all is said and done, I expect it will end up to be somewhere in the vicinity of three hundred and fifty thousand dollars. That's a conservative estimate. It could be more."

I gasp at the sheer magnitude of the number.

He's right. There's not even the slightest possibility my father will be able to repay him, and I'm not sure I'll ever be able to either. Certainly not in cash. "This will take some time, JD. I'll need a week. Maybe a month. Add additional interest to the debt. I don't care. I'll come up with the money."

"And how are you fixin' to do that?"

He's smug and comfortable, his long legs stretched out in front of him. I hear it in the informal cadence of his speech, the way his Ivy League education yields to his Southern roots. He asks the question like he already knows the answer. But I suppose only a fool wouldn't wonder how I expect to raise all that cash. JD is many things, but he's never been foolish. Calculating and clever, but never foolish. I doubt that's changed. "I'll go to the bank. And my fiancé will help."

When he says nothing, I glance up nervously.

His body is tight and a storm is brewing in his eyes. "Your fiancé is a worthless piece of shit who has about drained his bank account, and given the opportunity, would siphon every dime out of this place, too."

"You don't know a damn thing about my fiancé, or our relationship. So just stop."

"I know he hangs around sleazy bars on the dock, looking for a game to lay a bet on or a whore to stick his tiny dick into."

I swallow the humiliation and lift my chin. "I don't believe you."

"Suit yourself. You always liked fantasies."

JD edges forward in the chair, his arm resting on his thigh, his face closer to mine. "Think about what I'm offering," he murmurs. His fingertip trails a path from the crook of my elbow to my inner wrist, the callused pad rousing the sensitive skin. He hovers brazenly over my racing pulse. "Nervous? Or is it something else?"

I shiver and jerk my arm away, rubbing my hand up and down over the place where his has been, hoping to wipe away the sensation.

JD gets up and smooths his trousers with a ghost of a smile that mocks me.

He knows. He knows that no matter how much I hate him, my body hasn't forgotten. Even after all these years. It both shames and angers me, so I do what any well-raised Southern woman in my situation would do. I take a swing. Not with my fists, but with words, delivered in a syrupy voice dripping with sarcasm.

"You want me to be your whore? That's all you need from me? It really is no bother. Let's start right now." I make a big show of unzipping my boots and flinging them across the office, one at a time. Then I take off my jewelry, piece by piece.

While I'm behaving like a woman possessed, he's standing

with his back toward me, scrolling through his phone, completely unmoved. It's not until I slam my ivory bangle onto the desktop that he glances over one shoulder.

"Don't push me unless you want to end up bent over that desk with your skirt around your waist. I don't have the patience for it tonight. And stop acting like a petulant child. From what I remember, you're getting the best of the deal."

"Bastard," I spew, from somewhere deep and ugly.

He swivels to face me. "Unfortunately for you, darlin', I'm my father's son. Inherited every one of his despicable genes."

The hair at the back of my neck prickles. His father is a monster, and we both know it. I understand *exactly* the message JD's sending.

"Enough about me." He reaches down and encircles my wrist with one hand, pushing up the bell sleeve of my dress with the other, exposing the fading purple bruises on my upper arm where Dean grabbed me. "This is what I want to know about."

Long, embarrassing minutes pass while he examines each black and blue mark. The disgust on his face causes me more pain than the bruises.

"What happened?"

"I bumped into an armoire. It's nothing."

"Don't you lie to me. Those are finger marks on your skin."

I yank my arm in an effort to escape his hold, but he clenches my wrist tighter. Still, he doesn't dig painfully into the flesh the way Dean had. "It's none of your business."

He lets go of my wrist and I sit behind the desk, putting some distance between us.

But JD isn't finished.

He reaches over and unloops the scarf from around my neck, and before I think to secure it, it's in his hand. There's a long, angry hiss while he glares at the bruises on my throat. They're fading too, more green and yellow than purple, but they're still large and ghastly. I instinctively reach to cover them, but he swats my hand away.

His fingers skim my throat, lingering over each bruise. I squeeze my eyes tight, but a small tear escapes and slides down my cheek for him to see.

"Do they hurt?"

I shake my head. "Not anymore."

"I don't have all night and I'm not leaving before you tell me what happened."

"You knew exactly where to look for the bruises, so you already know what happened."

"I want to hear it from your mouth. All of it. The truth."

"He had too much to drink. It was only one time."

"*Only one time?* He choked you, Gabrielle. That's one fucking time too many." His voice is a whisper. A menacing whisper he's fighting to control.

It takes all the strength I have not to cower as the tremor of his barely restrained rage reverberates through the room.

"Did he hit you?"

My hands are trembling, and I clasp them on my lap to steady them. I didn't do anything wrong, but still, I feel small and ashamed. "You've seen the damage. Does it really matter?"

"Did. He. Hit. You?"

"Yes," I mutter.

JD takes half a step back and brushes a loose curl off my cheek. His touch is careful, gentle and warm, and my eyelids droop with a heavy flutter. "Did he force himself on you?" His voice is softer and kinder now, too, and for a moment I feel like he's the man I once knew and loved.

I shake my head. "No."

It's a lie. Another lie tumbling off the tongue of the woman who always chooses truth over lies. But I don't dare tell JD the truth about that night.

"I cannot believe that sonofabitch had his drunken hands

around your neck tight enough to leave those kinds of marks. He could have killed you." JD growls like a grizzly caught in a steel-jaw trap and stumbles back, running a hand over his head to the base of his neck. He squeezes the muscle a few times. Then swivels to face me.

"Tell me you love him," he demands. "Tell me you cling to him and scream his name when he fills your pussy. Go ahead, tell me." He's looming over me now, both hands planted on my desk, disgust oozing from every word. "You won't say it because you can't bear to hear the filthy lie come out of your own mouth." He drops the scarf in my lap. "And this is the man you expect to save you? This is the man you want to marry? What the hell is wrong with you, Gabrielle?"

My fingers find the scarf, rubbing the silky fabric between them for comfort.

"That relationship is over," he fumes.

I've had more than enough of the paternalistic attitude. "What do you mean, it's over? You can't—"

"I already did."

His words are final. Spoken as though what I think, what I care about, is of no importance. My anger mounts again. "What did you do, threaten to make him your bitch?"

He glares at me through squinted eyes and dismisses my question as though it's nothing. And in a way, it is nothing. Nothing more than an insolent remark requiring no serious response. I want to jab at him. That's all. I want to hurt him the way he hurt me.

He straightens and buttons his suit jacket. "I have a victory party to get to."

"Your father won?" The surprise in my voice is unmistakable. It was possible, but I never expected he would actually win. Not many people did. *God help us all.*

He nods, but his face gives nothing away.

Unless things have changed markedly, JD has little use for

his father. But still, I would have expected him to be more pleased about the outcome of the election. Instead of poisoning just South Carolina, the Wilders can now spread their special brand of misery all over the country.

Before he leaves, I need to put an end to this. And I make my final stand with as much bravado as I can muster. "I will not be your whore."

"I don't expect you to be my whore. You'll get as much pleasure from our arrangement as I will. Maybe more, if you can manage to stop snarling and calling me names long enough to enjoy it."

I don't know what I ever saw in him. He's nothing more than a vile, self-righteous hypocrite dressed in expensive clothing. And I want at him. I want it in the worst way.

"Lay it out, JD. Go ahead. You can stand there all high and mighty, but you're no different than Dean. You might not leave the kind of bruises that are visible to the eye, but don't think for one minute you're *any* better than him."

As soon as the words tumble off my tongue, he's towering over me, one hand gripping the back of my seat. He's trembling. I feel his rage through the bones of the chair. My heart thumps wildly, and I know the instant he spits out the first word, I pushed too far.

"Your mother gets the care she desperately needs to stay alive. Your father's debts are forgiven." He leans over, so close his breath heats my scalp, but it's not a soothing sensation. It's biting and bitter, like his words. "In exchange. You. Are. Mine. To enjoy as I like. Take it or leave it."

I glance up when he quiets. His face is screwed up with a fury I don't recognize. I'm the one trembling now, not in anger, but with fear.

Before I can calm myself, his shadow recedes, and he strides toward the door. My hands are balled so tight, the white-tipped nails leave bloody crescents on my palms.

He turns in the doorway. "The offer stands until tomorrow evening at eight."

I don't respond, and JD doesn't leave. Instead, he stands there, appraising me, as though he has more to say. I've already heard plenty from him, so I open my desk drawer and begin organizing the gel pens and index cards, sorting each by size and color.

"Gabrielle?"

I glance at him, and immediately wish I hadn't.

"If you breathe a single word about this to anyone, you'll watch in horror as your mother's body is ravaged by disease. You have my word."

For the first time in my life, I'm truly afraid of him. Terrified of the rage I unleashed. I knew better than to push and push, to compare him to a man like Dean, but I did it anyway.

"Antoine will meet you in the hotel lobby tomorrow at eight. We'll have supper at Sweetgrass and discuss the terms in more detail. I'll answer any questions you have. If you're not interested in what I'm offering, just send word with him, and I won't bother you again. I'm not forcing you to do this. Come willingly, or don't come at all. It's entirely up to you."

He saunters out of the office as though he hasn't just dropped a bomb on my world. As if I actually have a choice. Without thinking, I pick up a bud vase off my desk and hurl it at him through the doorway. It misses, hitting the corner of Georgina's desk. The vase shatters dramatically and water splashes onto his elegant suit, but he doesn't stop. Doesn't flinch. He just keeps walking.

READ JD and Gabrielle's second chance at love in **DEPRAVED**, https://amzn.to/42bNCA7

GREED EXCERPT

Chapter 1

DANIELA

GETTING through customs takes longer than expected, and by the time the taxi stops in front of the Moniz Law Office, light is breaking over the horizon.

"How much is the fare?" I ask, opening my wallet.

Before the driver answers, his phone rings. "One moment, please," he mutters, holding up a finger to silence me.

What's one more lost moment? It won't change anything—not for me. Although lingering at the curb isn't a good idea.

I adjust the hideous sunglasses from Dollar Mart and lower the brim on my cap before turning my face toward the sidewalk. It's not much of a disguise, but at this hour it's enough to get me from the car to the door without being recognized.

Once inside, I'll sign the paperwork transferring the property and return to the airport in time to catch a flight back to the US. If all goes according to plan, I'll be home before the end of the day, sleeping in my own bed tonight.

My own bed, *yes*. But Fall River isn't home. It's a safe harbor. The place where everyone important to me—everyone who's left—is awaiting my return. The gritty American city has been my refuge for the past six years, but it's not home.

I sigh deeply as the light creeps across the sky—purple hues melting into gold, casting a celestial glow on the ancient city, softening centuries of wear.

While I wait for the driver to end the call, I soak in every nuance, committing the smallest details to memory. It might be years before I see the sun rise over Porto again. *This could be the last time.*

As I untangle my emotions, a small box truck pulls in front of us.

The taxi headlights shine on the rear of the vehicle, illuminating the chain and padlock securing the roll-up door. From this angle, it's the single defining feature. The truck is so unremarkable it could fade seamlessly into the landscape, coming and going without catching anyone's attention.

My stomach roils as I study the grimy license plate.

Memorizing a series of numbers won't do you one bit of good if you're abducted.

I grab the door handle, prepared to bolt. But before I do, a delivery man emerges from the truck with three bags of sandwich rolls. He jogs across the street and drops the bread on a bench outside a shuttered coffee shop.

I draw a breath to quiet the trembling inside.

This might be home, but it's not safe for me here—and it might never be. I can't even begin to think about testing the waters until after Quinta Rosa do Vale officially changes hands, and the deed is sealed and recorded as a matter of public record.

After that, I'm not worth anything. Yes, I'll be millions of dollars richer, but money isn't what they want from me. It's the priceless vineyards. It's always been about the vineyards.

"How do you want to pay?" the driver asks, pointing to the charge on the taximeter.

"Euros. Thank you," I murmur, handing him some bills before getting out.

My eyes dart up and down the deserted street before I climb the steep steps into the building.

This is it. After I sign the papers, we'll be safe. No more looking over my shoulder. Despite the freedom ahead, a muscle in my chest contracts painfully.

I'm not sure the price of safety has ever been so high, but this isn't just about me. If it were, I'd never give up Quinta Rosa do Vale. They'd have to pry it from my cold, dead hands.

Inside the shallow entryway, I pause to offer a small prayer. Not to God—he doesn't seem to want any part of my dilemma —but to my parents, *to my mother*, who I hope will forgive me for what I'm about to do. In my shoes, she would do the same thing. At least that's what I tell myself when my conscience pricks sharply. Although it never dulls the pain. *How can it?*

When I sign those papers today, I'll be spitting on the graves of my ancestors. With a simple stroke of the pen, I'll convey more than three centuries of my family's blood, sweat, and tears to a stranger.

A stranger.

I still don't know the identity of the buyer. Attorney Moniz has been dealing with the representative of a trust. *The Iberian Trust.* But someone's hiding behind that trust—that's for damn sure.

The bile rises in my throat as I imagine the possibilities. In truth, a complete stranger is preferable to some of the alternatives my mind conjures.

I shove the cap and sunglasses into my tote, but I don't bother to even finger-comb my hair. Who cares if I look like hell? *Nobody.* In less than an hour, I'll be nothing more than a tragic footnote in the history of the region.

When I step into the lobby, a young woman in a smart blue dress is at the reception desk. I don't remember her, but it's been six years since I was last here. *Shortly after my eighteenth birthday.* I'm sure a lot has changed. *Like I have.*

She looks up as I approach. "Good morning."

"Good morning. I have an appointment with Attorney Moniz. Daniela D'Sousa," I add, just above a whisper, as though my name alone might summon demons from the rafters.

"Of course, Ms. D'Sousa," she says kindly. "He told me to send you right up when you arrive. Do you know where his office is located?"

"Is it still at the top of the staircase, across from the library?"

"Yes." She nods, adjusting the brooch on her silk scarf. "I think he might still be on a call, but if the door is open, go right in and take a seat."

I turn toward the stairs, but a sense of unease stops me in my tracks. "Is Attorney Moniz alone?"

Moniz assured me the buyer wouldn't be here. *"It's too early for the civilized to do business, and it will be easier for you this way."* But circumstances can change, and I don't want to be caught off guard.

"At this hour?" The receptionist's blonde head bobs up and down as she smiles reassuringly. "Can I bring you some coffee or tea?"

"Tea would be wonderful. Thank you."

I breathe a small sigh of relief and find the stairs. Pedro Moniz, my father's lawyer and old friend, made this long, tortuous process, mired in arcane Portuguese property law, as easy as possible for me.

Although there was nothing he could say or do to blunt the heartache.

The paintings in the stairwell are the same ones that have hung here since I was a child. The Douro Valley's most important churches, port houses, and vineyards captured on canvas for all to admire.

I squeeze the railing and lower my gaze before I get to the painting of Quinta Rosa do Vale.

It's a stunning piece of art, painted right before harvest, when the grapes were plump, their purple skins pulled tight over the sweet flesh.

I can't bear to look at it.

One foot in front of the other, Daniela. It's almost over.

When I reach the top, Moniz's door is open, but the lights are off. Apart from the hissing and groaning of a radiator awakening, it's quiet. *Too quiet.*

Maybe he's finished with the call. Or perhaps he's taking it from one of the other rooms.

The receptionist said to go in and have a seat.

I clutch my tote and step timidly across the threshold into the dark office. At first, it appears I'm alone. But as my eyes adjust, I notice a man at the window in the far corner of the room. He's gazing at the sunrise with a phone to his ear.

As the shadowy figure comes into focus, the hair on the back of my neck rises. Even with his back to me, even in the dim light, even after all this time, I recognize him immediately.

A warning blares inside my head, and I turn to flee. But the doorway is blocked by the man who sat behind me on the plane—the hulking giant who looks like he plays American football for a professional team.

I can't breathe.

"Excuse me, please," I plead, as though he might let me by if I'm polite.

The hulk doesn't utter a word or spare me even a small glance, and he doesn't budge. But I'm desperate to leave before the man at the window notices me, and I attempt to muscle my way through.

It's a waste of energy. He's an unmovable force.

When I pivot to find an alternate exit, Antonio Huntsman is there, eyes flaring, almost daring me to run, again.

———

Chapter 2

DANIELA

I FREEZE IN MY TRACKS, a cornered animal with little hope for survival.

He's still too, intensely focused, like a predator who could be easily triggered.

It's been years since I've seen him in person, but the younger version of this man still haunts my dreams—more often than I care to admit.

The last time we were this close, he stole a kiss. That's what I tell myself, because it's easier than admitting I gave it to him— that I wanted that kiss.

Twenty minutes after the reckless kiss, his car was forced off the road, into the river. When I left Porto, he was in critical condition, and it was unclear whether he would survive.

But it's hard to kill the devil.

He doesn't look any worse for wear. In many ways, he looks the same. Maybe more confident. The intensity still vibrates off him in a way that signals danger. *Beautiful danger. Irresistible danger.* The kind that beckons, not with a word but with a smoldering gaze.

Standing here, with his hand buried in his trouser pocket, he's a photographer's dream.

Venomous snakes always hide under pretty skins.

I continue to hold myself as still as possible, only swallowing to clear my airway.

"Our fate—yours and mine—is entwined for eternity. For now, you're safe, Princesa. But when I come back, it'll be for more than a kiss." Those were his last words to me.

The door clicks shut behind me, cutting off more of my air supply.

"Where's Moniz?" I gasp, my voice barely audible.

"I gave him the morning off." Antonio gestures toward one of the chairs near the desk. "Have a seat, Daniela."

His commanding tenor raises gooseflesh on my arms.

He knows you're here to sell the property. He wants it.

Sit and hear him out, or stand and fight. Those are my choices.

My soul shrivels at the thought of a Huntsman owning my mother's vineyards.

You're not in a position to be sentimental. Especially now. Don't waste time pretending you won't sell to him. You'll do what you need to do so you can get back to Isabel and Valentina.

Maybe I can negotiate something, because between him and the guard stationed outside the door, I don't think fighting is going to get me far.

I lower myself to the edge of the seat, using the chair's sturdy arm for support. "I assume this is about the vineyards."

He shakes his head, unbuttoning his suit jacket before propping himself on the corner of the desk, where he can lord over me like a king.

"I have a plane to catch and no time for games. What is this about?"

He doesn't reply, but he looks me up and down, suggestively, his eyes lingering here and there without a tinge of shame. It's much the way he leered when he visited after my father died. It's still appalling, but this time, I don't blink.

Six long years have passed since that visit, and in the

interim, my life has shifted, dramatically. Instead of having an entire staff to help me with tedious chores, I'm now the maid. Rather than a lavish wing to myself, I share a bedroom with a child. Not a single person treats me like I'm from an important Portuguese family—they don't even know, and if they did, they wouldn't care.

Some might see this fall from grace as a tragedy, others as my comeuppance. I don't have the energy to conduct a thorough analysis. At the end of the day, I do what's necessary to keep food on the table and a roof over our heads. It's a simple, sometimes grueling life, but it's kept us safe.

When Antonio completes his lewd appraisal, his dark, piercing eyes meet mine. It's a look designed to intimidate. And it does. But despite the intermittent tremor in my left eye, I don't shrink—that would only empower him.

The old radiator gurgles in the corner. Otherwise, the room is deathly quiet. The air between us so heavy, it's practically weeping. Antonio's scrutiny is hard and threatening, without a glimmer of humanity.

My hands are beginning to ache from being clasped so tightly, but at least they're not shaking.

I don't know his intentions, but I can guess. This is about the vineyards. *It has to be.*

There's a binding contract on the property. *You're too late, Antonio.*

Although it's never too late for wealthy, powerful men to get their way. It's either handed to them at the very last minute, or they snatch it from unwitting hands. There's rarely a penalty for that kind of behavior, so they walk away unscathed and emboldened. And they do it again, and again, because the greedy are insatiable.

I glance at him. His expression hasn't softened—if anything, it's more menacing. More determined.

Antonio is about to make my life a living hell. It's written all over him, twisting in his sharp features, scraping through the vast silence—metal against metal. I feel it in my bones. A chill so pervasive that a hot bath and layers of spun wool won't cure it.

"Why are you here?" I ask softly, my voice straining under the stress.

He doesn't reply. He hasn't said a single word since he told me to have a seat. For now, he seems content to let my anxiety build.

The wait is making me jittery. Inside, the threads are spooling tighter and tighter. Soon they'll snap, and my emotions will spin out of control. I can't allow it to happen.

I know pain. Torn flesh, bitter anguish, heartache—I know the demons intimately. Even more, I know how to battle through the suffering.

Yes, I might end up bloodied and scarred, but Antonio Huntsman can't throw anything at me I can't handle.

I sit up taller and dig in my heels. "What do you want?"

This time, there's not a shred of softness or deference in my tone. It's insistent and demanding, leaving no doubt that I'll ask again, and again, until he answers the question.

His gaze narrows, zeroing in on mine with laser focus. "It's time to come home, Daniela."

His voice is firm. Uncompromising. And while I doubt anyone ever says *no* to him, his jaw is set, as though he's bracing for a fight.

This isn't at all what I expected. I assumed he got wind of the sale and would demand I breach the contract with the buyer and sell him the property instead.

The butterflies in my stomach swirl frantically while I try to form a coherent response that won't back me farther into a corner.

"I don't understand." I choose the words carefully, feigning ignorance, although it's not much of a stretch. I really don't know where he's headed.

"Porto is your home. You belong here. This is your legacy."

It takes me long moments to wrap my head around it. But when I finally do, it feels as though my soul has been exposed to the light, filleted with surgical precision.

Porto is your home. You belong here. This is your legacy.

If I didn't know better, I would think the bastard is privy to my dreams—my ridiculous fantasies. The ones I never share with anyone. Not even Isabel. Dreams that are so far out of reach, the edges are fuzzy.

He knows the property is changing hands today. Of course he does. Despite Moniz's efforts to conceal the sale, that shouldn't come as a total surprise. But he also knows what's in my heart. He knows how much I want to keep Quinta Rosa do Vale, how much I want to come home, back to my old life, and he's using that knowledge to play me in the cruelest way.

He wants me to come home. *Bullshit. He wants the vineyards. Don't let him lure you off the path. It's not safe.*

I look straight into his eyes. All these years of hiding have taught me to lie without squirming. "My home is in Canada now, with my great-aunt. She needs me." It's the same lie I told last time to throw him off my trail. But I went directly to the US, without ever setting foot in Canada.

Antonio wraps his long fingers around the beveled edge of the desk and angles forward ever so slightly.

"Really?"

His tone is smug. So smug I'd like to slap him across the face hard enough to make my palm sting.

"What does she need? Someone to water the flowers around her grave?"

He knows she's dead. Why would he bother with my relatives? Why?

I lower my eyes, giving myself a few seconds to regroup.

———

Chapter 3

DANIELA

IF HE KNOWS about my great-aunt, what else does he know?

I imagine him digging into the past, unearthing secrets meant to remain buried forever.

I'm so worked up I can't think straight, and a few measly seconds isn't enough to clear my head.

It doesn't matter who buys the property. *But it does. No, it doesn't. Not anymore. You're out of options. He knows the deal is almost done, and he's not going to allow the sale unless it's to him. Remember who you left back in the US. That's your only concern now.*

"I've entered into a sales agreement with a buyer," I blurt when the voices arguing inside my head become too much. "We've been working on the sale for several years, but I'm willing to sell you the vineyards, if you can persuade the buyer to let me out of the contract."

I despise myself right now. My cowardice. My unwillingness to fight for something that rightfully belongs to me. But I hate him even more. I hate him with every fiber of my being.

"The employees need to be treated fairly," I add, modulating my voice to hide how much I loathe him. "A strong severance package, or better, they'll be allowed to keep their jobs. The contract I came to sign protects everyone who works at Quinta Rosa do Vale. That's all I care about."

"That's all you care about? You don't care if I torch the house you grew up in, or the vineyards your family nurtured for generations? The vineyards that provide grapes to make the Port that keeps the entire region afloat? And you don't care about money for yourself? Is that right?"

What a prick.

But I can deal with it. My new life has made me stronger and, to some extent, tougher. It's taught me how much the human spirit can bend to survive. The universe already taught me that lesson once, but I was too young to grasp it fully at the time. Now I could write a thesis on it.

I'm a survivor. Plain and simple. Antonio Huntsman's bullying doesn't even nick the surface.

It takes some doing, but I gather the courage to respond.

"I can live without your money. And the region will manage without Quinta Rosa do Vale's grapes. But if you want to burn the property to the ground, be my guest. I'm not going to stop you. To be clear, I'd rather see it in a mountain of ashes than with your family."

His closely groomed beard doesn't hide the tic in his jaw.

"Tough words from a woman confined to the four corners of this room. If I were you, I'd be pleading for mercy instead of trying to piss me off."

In the US, I'm a woman struggling to make ends meet, like so many others. There's nothing unique about me. But here, I'm still a D'Sousa. And I'll be damned before I beg a Huntsman for anything.

"You're going to do what you want to do," I reply coolly. "You're going to take what you want to take. Pleading for mercy doesn't work with men like you." *I've seen it firsthand.* "I'm not getting on my knees for the likes of you."

He crosses his arms over his broad chest and sits back. But his scowl doesn't recede.

"Work it out with the buyer. I'll sign whatever you want," I assure him, standing. "But I've got a plane to catch, so if you'll excuse me."

"Sit down," he growls. "We're done when I say we're done. Not one second sooner."

His voice is low, laced with simmering rage.

I don't sit. Not because I want to challenge him—although I do—but my better sense tells me he's too angry to push any further. I don't sit because the stress and the jet lag are catching up with me. My body feels like it's running seconds behind my brain.

"You will sit in that chair by your own accord, or with my assistance, but you will do it."

He shifts his leg, and I collapse into the seat before he makes good on the threat.

His father had no reservations about raising his hand to a woman. *Children learn what they live.* I highly doubt Antonio Huntsman is above manhandling me.

"I don't know what more you want from me."

I sound beaten, and in many ways, I am.

"You're in a better position to work it out with the buyer," I explain, although he knows it. "You have more influence, more lawyers, more money. I have nothing but the property—that I've already agreed, in writing, to sell."

"The buyer? Iberian Trust?" He peers down at me with an expression that seems less hostile now.

I nod.

"That trust belongs to the Huntsman portfolio."

At first I don't understand what he's talking about. I'm exhausted. I haven't slept well in weeks, and I didn't sleep a wink on my overnight flight. My brain churns slowly as it tries to make sense of it. Then it dawns on me. It was here, in front of me, all along.

I should have known. *Moniz should have known.*

The question I have for him is within easy grasp. It's right there, but when I open my mouth, nothing comes out. It's as though my tongue has been immobilized, swaddled in layers of dusty cotton.

It takes considerable effort, but eventually I manage to eke out the words without choking. "You're the buyer?"

Antonio shakes his head. "I'm not a buyer. The paperwork is a sham. Quinta Rosa do Vale already belongs to me." He reaches down and takes a lock of my hair between his fingers. "As do you."

I jerk away from his touch, but his grip tightens until my scalp screams. At first the pain is welcome, cutting through a growing numbness. But soon the throb becomes too much, and I'm forced to sit still while he fingers my hair. *Still, but not quiet.*

"What the hell are you talking about?" I snarl, the hatred eclipsing the fear in my heart.

"Both you and the vineyards have been mine since the moment your father took his last breath. And Daniela, you will get on your knees for me. Make no mistake about it."

———

Chapter 4

DANIELA

THE BASTARD ISN'T TALKING about kneeling in prayer. *What a monster.*

You expected something different from the son of o diabo?

No. Not really. But the foolish girl inside remembers Antonio differently. At least she wants to remember him differently.

If you listen to her, she'll lead you to danger. It's true. She will.

"I want to speak to Pedro Moniz."

Antonio releases his grip on my hair and sits back, his long fingers drumming on the desk. "Moniz is my attorney. It's unlikely he'll talk to you about my business matters. Not if he wants to live long enough to play with his pretty young wife tonight."

Oh my God. Moniz was in on the whole thing. It was an ambush. I walked right into the trap without even a whiff of their scheme.

How could my father's closest friend have sold me out like this? I've known him all my life. He was at my birthday parties and at the church for my First Communion. He would come on Christmas and eat at our table and share our wine. He held my hand while my father passed.

Papai trusted him. He told me to trust Moniz too. *"Pedro knows everything about my business matters. Don't hesitate to go to him for advice. He'll guide you wisely, Daniela."*

The traitorous bastard guided me, all right. Straight into the wolf's lair.

I should have known better.

Pedro Moniz belongs to my father's world—Antonio's world. The old boys' club that controls *everything* in Porto. I'm a woman. A *young* woman. *And clearly naive.* Even if Antonio wasn't a threat, Moniz would never betray the silent oath that binds powerful men—*not even for me.*

"*Quinta Rosa do Vale already belongs to me. As do you.*"

My heart is pounding so hard I'm certain he can see it through my jacket. *I need a plan.* A foolproof one. And I need it now.

I dig into my tote for some balm and glide it over my lips as he watches quietly. Chapped lips are the least of my worries, but it buys me a little time.

Maybe, *maybe*, he owns the property—I'll need to see proof —but this is the twenty-first century, and human beings cannot be owned like pets. *Not even in Porto.*

I can't come up with a viable plan. *Nothing.* All I can do is draw this out, hoping that something will come to me—before it's too late.

"I have no idea what you're talking about."

His eyes blaze as he speaks. *The victor with the spoils in reach.* "Your father bequeathed me the property on the condition I marry you. It's time for me to make good on my end of the deal."

Every inch of me is numb. Inside and out. It's almost as though he's speaking in tongues, using words and phrases no mortal can comprehend.

I'm a pawn in a deal. Chattel for barter.

My father arranged my marriage—*to a Huntsman.* The very people responsible for my mother's torture and death. *Papai* loved her with every piece of his heart. Every single one. And he loved me. I'm sure of it.

I glance up at Antonio. His eyes are soft, and I see what looks like pity in his expression. But no regret. There's nothing that even resembles regret or remorse, and he's certainly not seeking forgiveness. Men like him never seek forgiveness. Not even with their last breath.

If I want to be free of him, I need to appeal not to his heart or conscience, but to his practical sense. Because in the end he'll do what's best for him.

"You don't want to marry me."

The corner of his mouth lifts slyly. "Not any more than you want to marry me. Maybe less."

Could he be more of an asshole?

"Here's the truth, Daniela. Even if frivolous emotions were part of my nature, I would never marry for love. When I take a wife, it will be strictly a business decision. You were offered to me with a priceless piece of property." He shrugs. "Why not you?"

I swallow hard, my insides quivering.

His tone is emotionally bankrupt. Devoid of all passion— let alone anything approximating love. It's chilling. Even if he wanted me just for sex, it would feel more humane. This is a cold, calculated business decision. *One I had no voice in.*

I don't know what my father was thinking.

Papai knew my pain. He never invited Antonio to our home while I was there—not until he was dying, and then only that one time. My father knew the risks involved with marrying into the Huntsman family—especially when he was gone and couldn't protect us. I can't believe that, in the end, he chose this for me. That he would take this kind of risk. I don't believe it.

"My father would never arrange a marriage between your family and mine."

The words come from my mouth, but I almost don't recognize myself speaking. It's as though I'm standing outside my body, watching the events of my life unfold. *Disassociating.* I've never had therapy, but I've learned a lot about trauma. The last time I experienced something like this, I was twelve. *Maybe I haven't toughened up.*

"We're going to have serious problems," he warns, "if you don't start trusting my word."

"We already have serious problems." My voice is flat and hollow, reflecting the defeat I feel inside.

Antonio raps his knuckles on the polished desk. "The circumstances are unique, and I imagine this news comes as a shock."

A shock? A shock is when wet fingers touch a live wire. This is ripping my beating heart from my chest and stomping on it.

"I'll humor you, today," he adds, like he's doing me a big favor. "But this will be the last time I provide evidence to back up my word. And it will be the last time you accuse me of being a liar."

He hands me a laminated sheet of paper from the desk. "That should address your concerns."

I stare at the page. At first, the individual letters are all I see.

The black lines and swirls blending into one another. Eventually I begin to make out words.

It's a simple contract. One sheet of paper, front and back, signed by Huntsman and my father. My heart clenches at *Papai*'s familiar scrawl.

Near each signature, there's a small mahogany spatter. I draw a deep breath to steady my trembling hand. The stain is a drop of each man's blood. I'm certain of it.

A blood oath.

My chest aches.

Unless this is another sham, I'm screwed.

READ DANIELA and Antonio's epic love story in **GREED** https://amzn.to/3Bbp4vS

A FINAL WORD FROM EVA

I hope you loved Carnal Vengeance! It's been so much fun creating the Bourbon Dynasty series and planning for a big February release (although I expect the series to release in January—*Shhh!* don't tell anyone!) We have so many exciting things planned for the launch. I hope you'll be a part of our celebration!

You can find Tainted King on Amazon, **https://www.amazon.com/dp/BoD1VW63YR**

For up-to-date information about me and my work, sneak peeks, exclusive giveaways, and fun, I invite you to join my VIP Newsletter at **www.evacharles.com** AND my FB reader group JD's Closet.

xoxo
Eva

ABOUT THE AUTHOR

Eva Charles is the *USA Today* bestselling author of steamy romantic suspense with dangerous billionaires and strong heroines.

When she's not writing, trying to squeeze information out of her tight-lipped sons, or playing with the two naughtiest dogs you've ever met, Eva's creating chapters in her own love story.

Sign-up for my monthly newsletter for FREE story in the Sinful Empire world!
www.evacharles.com

I'd love to hear from you!
eva@evacharles.com

MORE STEAMY ROMANTIC SUSPENSE BY EVA CHARLES

BOURBON DYNASTY

Carnal Vengeance

Tainted King

Scarlet Queen

Righteous Reign

A SINFUL EMPIRE SERIES

TRILOGY (COMPLETE)

Greed

Lust

Envy

DUET (COMPLETE)

Pride

Wrath

THE DEVIL'S DUE (SERIES COMPLETE)

Depraved

Delivered

Bound

Decadent

CONTEMPORARY ROMANCE

NEW AMERICAN ROYALS

Sheltered Heart

Noble Pursuit

Double Play

Unforgettable

Loyal Subjects

Sexy Sinner

Made in the USA
Middletown, DE
03 May 2024

53805495R00081